With Madog
to the New World

WITH
MADOG
TO THE NEW
WORLD

dina▲

J. MALCOLM PRYCE

Also by Malcolm Price:

A Dragon to Agincourt

£7.95

0 862433 842

Cover: Welsh Books Council

ISBN: 0 86243 758 X

Dinas is an imprint of Y Lolfa

Published and printed in Wales by
Y Lolfa Cyf., Talybont, Ceredigion SY24 5AP
e-mail ylolfa@ylolfa.com
website www.ylolfa.com
tel. (01970) 832 304
fax 832 782

1

1820 AD

Zebediah Carter's paddle broke its steady rhythm as his canoe's bow cleared a wide bend in the river. Less than two hundred yards ahead, on the left bank, stood a large Indian village, the domed roofs of the lodges standing out like giant mushrooms against the green prairie. Yet, it was not the buildings that caused him to falter, but the sight of some twenty warriors who stood at the water's edge watching the canoe's approach. Sensing the back end of the light craft break away, he dug his paddle deeply into the water and risked a quick glance over his shoulder.

'Keep paddling, Caleb,' he called out. 'Gotter face them out. After all is said, they's the reason we are here.'

At the rear of the canoe, Caleb Evans took another quick look at the gathered Indians, then obeyed his partner's command. Thrusting his wooden blade into the river at an angle, he corrected the craft's drift, and then paddled strongly forward. At this point the Missouri ran shallow but swiftly in its long journey south, and as the canoe crept slowly toward the village, his mind flitted quickly back over the past few weeks.

He had met up with Zeb, purely by chance, in the frontier town of St. Louis. The older man was planning a trip that would take him further than any other trader had so far been, and had welcomed Caleb's offer of company.

'Ye may be a greenhorn,' he'd chuckled, 'but yuv made it this far west and yer still in good shape; 'sides which, I need another paddler.'

Pooling every cent he possessed with Zeb's cash, they had purchased enough provisions for their journey. With the balance, the trader had bartered hard for the ironware that now lay in the bottom of the canoe. By now, he had every confidence in Zeb's knowledge of the wilderness, but he could not resist the urge to peek under the canvas sheet that protected their belongings and cargo, to check the two muskets that lay there side by side. His concern, however, was soon dispelled. As the bottom of the canoe scraped against gravel, half a dozen warriors leapt into the shallows and began to drag the light craft ashore. Caleb had scarcely time to note that the copper brown faces were smiling in welcome, before their craft lay firmly on the beach. Following Zeb's example, he scrambled out onto dry land and walked up to his partner's side.

'Now, lad, let's hope our luck holds,' Zeb said, holding an open hand in the air. 'From what tribe are you?' he called out, using the language of the Lakotan peoples.

'We are of the Mandan tribe,' an elderly Indian answered, stepping to the forefront. 'What do you want of us?'

'Our luck's in, Caleb,' Zeb said in an aside. 'They speak Lakotan, like some of the other tribes along the river.'

Taking a step closer to the Indian, he pointed towards the east.

'We have travelled from where the sun rises,' he answered. 'We are Americans and have come here to trade with you for furs.'

The old warrior put out a hand and gently stroked Zeb's beard, his eyes widening with surprise.'

It truly is your own hair,' he said, in amazement. 'I have heard of you people; you have pale skin. Is this not so?'

''Tis true enough,' Zeb answered. 'See for yourself.'

With a wide grin, he pulled up his woollen shirt to expose his torso, the white skin contrasting with his weathered face and forearms. The warriors gasped with astonishment then jostled each other as they tried to touch the trader.

'Enough,' their spokesman cried out. 'This is not the way to greet visitors to our village. I am Lone Elk, the peace chief of these people,' he said to Zeb, as the warriors drew back. 'You are welcome here. When the sun goes down, you will join us in a feast to celebrate your coming. You will stay in my lodge.'

His tone was one of command, and he began to stride towards the lodges, followed by Zeb. Grabbing the two muskets and powder horns, Caleb hurried after them, surrounded by the curious Indians, studying his escort as they walked along. To a man, they were tall and well built, wearing their long hair in braids, which came down over each shoulder. While some were clad in buckskin shirts and breeches, the majority wore no more than a breechclout, and it was amongst these that Caleb saw something that caused him to halt for a moment. Here and there amongst the press of warriors, there were men whose skin was fairer than that of the others. One of these noticed Caleb's stare and smiled back at him. The man's face was rounder, and his cheekbones less pronounced than those of his darker companions, and though smiling, his mouth was noticeably smaller. The young trader smiled in return, then, shrugging his shoulders with bewilderment, he hurried after his partner.

On entering the Chief's lodge, he was surprised to find a sense of order in the spacious building. The area closest to the low entrance, with a scattering of buffalo hides and rush mats laid on the packed earth floor, was obviously for day use. In the centre, a ring of stones held a glowing fire, the little smoke that it emitted escaping through a hole in the roof. Behind this, a semicircle of sleeping benches made from saplings ran around the wall, with robes arranged amongst them. Lone Elk motioned the two white men to two of these, then looked questioningly at the muskets when Caleb laid them down, though made no mention of them when he spoke.

'You are hungry?' he asked. 'For now, eat what my women have ready.'

He spoke briefly to one of the women who sat beside the entrance and she ladled out two bowlfuls of stewed meat and maize, which she handed to the traders. The Chief watched her do this then made to leave.

'Many of our people are away on a hunt,' he told them. 'They will return today, so I must make sure that all is prepared to greet them.'

'What about our goods, Zeb?' Caleb asked when the Chief had departed. 'We're taking a hell of a chance, leaving them unattended.'

'They are safe enough,' Zeb answered. 'Injuns ain't thieves. But, should one of them be tempted, he will offer us something in return. It's a kind of trading, I guess.'

Their meal eaten, Zeb lit his pipe and puffed away in contentment for a few minutes, then led the way outside.

'Let's go take a look around,' he said, ducking through the low entry. 'Keep an eye peeled for beaver pelts, Caleb. They are what makes the money back in Saint Louis.'

The two walked slowly through the village, pausing whenever they came to one of the wooden frames used for curing the pelts. Most of the skins were wolf or fox, though they did see the odd beaver here and there. Their progress was greeted with friendly cries whenever they drew close to any group of Indians, and Caleb noticed that quite a few of the squaws were fair skinned.

'Yep, I've noticed it myself,' Zeb replied, when Caleb remarked on the oddity, 'Sure got me beat. Some of those bucks on the river bank looked almost American, if it weren't for their hair.'

They had almost completed their tour, when they heard a

loud, whooping cry from outside the village and saw those about them begin to hurry towards the sound. Following them, the traders came out onto the open ground that led to the prairie. To their left and right, the Indians had cultivated the ground and they could see that this held stands of maize and millet. The source of the noise was a group of some forty mounted warriors, who raced their ponies in a wide circle, calling out to the gathering spectators. To Caleb, they made a magnificent picture as they raced past on their painted mounts, whooping and brandishing their lances or bows. Through a growing cloud of dust, he could see that two riders sat motionless within the circle, and, as he watched, one of these raised an arm high. Within moments, the warriors had brought their ponies to a halt and, now silent, they parted to allow the two to ride forward.

Drawing rein before Lone Elk, who had stepped clear of the crowd, they spoke with him, and Caleb saw the taller of the arrivals point westward. Looking in that direction, he now saw a column of people moving slowly over the prairie towards the village.

'Looks like their hunt is over,' Zeb commented. 'I wonder what luck they had.' His question was answered when the procession drew closer, for they could see that the horse drawn travois were laden with joints of buffalo meat. The sight brought shouts of joy from the watching crowd, and they were soon busily engaged in sharing the meat between everyone. The traders were still watching the scene when Lone Elk approached them, accompanied by the two other Indians. The appearance of the taller of these brought a gasp of surprise from Caleb. The man stood at least two inches over six feet in height, while his build told of enormous strength, yet it was his features that made the most impact. He had a large-boned face, similar to the Mandans, yet his braided hair was a light brown and his eyes were blue. His companion's appearance was similar to the lighter coloured

9

warriors that made up so much of the tribe, yet this man had a quiet air of authority about him. The traders and hunters studied each other for a while, before Lone Elk spoke out.

'This is White Eagle, Chief of all the Mandan people,' he said, gesturing to the smaller warrior. 'The other, Broken Lance, is our leader in war.'

The big man spoke to the Peace Chief, who replied at some length, while White Eagle continued his close scrutiny, although listening to what was being said. When finally the two Indians fell silent, he spoke for the first time.

'You are welcome to trade with my people,' he said, 'though you will find that we are experienced in this matter and are shrewd bargainers.' He smiled warmly at the white men, as though to soften his warning, then spoke on.

'We have heard of you people from our neighbours, the Cherokees, who live to the east. They say that you come from a land that lies on the other side of a great water. Did you travel over this in your canoe?'

Troubled though he was by the range of words, Zeb was able to get the gist.

'Not me,' he answered. 'I come from a place called Virginia. I ain't ever seen the ocean, as they call it, but my friend here has, though he were but a child at the time. What's the name of your homeland, Caleb?' he asked his partner.

'I was born in a country called Wales,' Caleb answered, puzzled by the unexpected question, 'though my folks call it Cymru.'

The next moment, he took an involuntary step backward, as White Eagle made to take hold of him.

'What the hell have I said?' he demanded of Zeb.

'Beats me, son,' his partner answered, 'but I don't think he means you any harm.'

'Ask your friend if this Cymru has many mountains and

rivers,' the Chief asked Zeb.

'According to Ma, it had plenty of both,' Caleb answered. 'She reckons it is a beautiful place but very poor and the people unhappy. She and Pa came over with a boatload of Welsh people who wanted a better life.'

Zeb translated what he could of this for the Chief, who listened intently to the words.

'There will be a feast when the sun goes to sleep,' he said. 'I will speak more to your friend then.'

Accompanied by the other two Indians, White Eagle led his pony into the village while Zeb and Caleb watched the scene around the travois. It was while they were doing this that it became clear that the Mandans consisted of three groups of people. There were those who, like Lone Elk, were definitely of Lakotan stock, others who looked similar to White Eagle, and some who were of the same build and colouring as Broken Lance. The two things they all had in common were their dress and language.

'They sure are a strange bunch,' Zeb remarked, when finally the two returned to the village.

That evening, as promised, a feast was held to celebrate the successful hunt. The two traders sat outside Lone Elk's lodge, where the Chiefs and their respective wives joined them. The women immediately began to help those already engaged in preparing a meal, while the men smoked a pipe of peace. After this ceremony, Lone Elk produced a clay pot, which he offered to White Eagle. The Chief raised the pot eagerly to his lips, drank deeply of its contents, then, wiping his mouth, he handed the pot to Broken Lance. Grinning with anticipation, the big Indian tipped his head back and drank, his Adam's apple moving slowly up and down. Still smiling broadly, he passed the pot to Zeb.

'This is a good drink, friend,' he said in a deep voice. 'Take what you will, for Lone Elk has more.'

He waited until the two white men had drunk, then he leaned closer to them.

'I have heard that you pale faces carry long sticks which sound like thunder and kill your enemies. Is it true? Do you have such weapons?'

''Tis true enough,' Zeb answered. 'We do have guns, though I only use mine for huntin'.'

'Then, show me,' Broken Lance said, in a voice which was full of command.

Rather reluctantly, Zeb entered the lodge, to return carrying his musket and powder horn, which he handed to the Indian. Broken Lance held the gun gingerly, feeling its weight, before squinting down the barrel, then looking enquiringly at the trader. Zeb fumbled in the pouch attached to his waist belt, and, drawing out a moulded bullet, tossed it over to the Indian.

'That's what does the killing,' he said.

The Indian rolled the bullet around in his cupped hand for a few seconds, then thrust the gun back at him.

'Show me how,' he demanded.

Zeb took the musket from him and ensured that the hammer was not cocked and that the frizzen was closed. Measuring a load of powder from the horn, he poured it down the barrel then inserted a piece of wadding, before ramming the charge home with the rod. Priming the pan, he looked over at the War Chief and shook his head.

'No kill now,' he said firmly.

With no more ado, he pointed the long barrel skyward, cocked the musket and squeezed the trigger. The resulting bang caused the women to scream with fright, while the Chiefs dived for cover. For a terrible few moments, in which he wondered if the Indians would turn ugly, there was a crushing silence. Then, to his relief, Broken Lance scrambled to his feet and burst out laughing.

'Wagh!' the big Indian exclaimed. 'What a fine weapon that is. Truly, a man could frighten his enemies to death.'

His face still beaming, he waved away the warriors who came running to the lodge.

'All is well,' he assured them. 'The white man has only been showing me his powerful medicine.'

When the commotion had died down, the women began to serve the feast. Their offering started with the liver and heart from a buffalo, rarely cooked, and then followed these with prime ribs of meat. They then sat apart from their men folk, who ate ravenously at first, though their hunger eased as the meal progressed. As promised, Lone Elk refilled the drinking pot and, to Caleb's surprise, he found that he was as eager as the others were to raise it to his lips. The smell from the brew was rather unsavoury, but that apart, the sweet, sour taste of the liquid made him wish for more.

It was well into the night when White Eagle got to his feet and made to leave.

'You and I must speak of your homeland another day,' he said to Caleb, slurring his words. 'I wish to know more of the place, but for now, my head is too fuddled.'

Zeb translated this as best he could as the Chief led the other guests from the lodge. Caleb's brain was also feeling the effect of Lone Elk's brew, and gladly he swayed over to his place on the bench. Not bothering to undress, he simply flopped down and closed his eyes. The day had been a long one and its events had taken their toll. Within seconds, he was sound asleep, blissfully unaware of the snores around him.

The subdued chatter of women's voices roused him from his slumber though he lay still, reluctant to move. Now and then one of the women would whisper something to her companions, which caused them to titter quietly amongst themselves, and after one such episode, Caleb's curiosity got the better of him. Opening his eyes, he felt a stab of alarm and sat quickly upright, the sudden movement sending a pounding through his skull. The cause of his fright was an unexpected face very close to his own. Its owner, a girl of some sixteen years, drew back in equal alarm, smiling nervously at him. Holding his throbbing head in both hands, he slid off the bench, noting that Zeb lay flat on his back, still asleep. The girl's companions greeted him in Lakotan, their faces split in wide grins. Caleb nodded gently in return, then, aware of a call of nature, ducked outside the lodge. The first Indian he saw was Lone Elk, who was seated dejectedly on a log, his face a picture of misery. Crossing over to him, Caleb made a motion with his hand, which explained his difficulty as clearly as any words. In answer, the old man smiled wanly then got to his feet, motioning the young trader to follow him. Their way led out of the village before turning downstream, where a. large clump of aspen followed the river's course. The Indian came to a halt, pointing at the trees and saying something in his guttural tongue. Caleb nodded his thanks and hurried ahead, his bowels rumbling ominously.

Ten minutes later, he rejoined the Peace Chief, who now led him back upstream. Above another bend in the river, the waters had shaped the gravel to form a pool some four feet deep, and here Lone Elk stripped off his buckskin and moccasins, and then plunged in. Although the day was yet young, the air was already warm, and Caleb found the sight irresistible, so, undressing, he followed suit. The shock of the cold water took his breath away for a few moments but then, as he began to swim, a feeling of sheer joy swept over him. The two men, Indian and American, behaved as children for some minutes, frolicking and laughing at each other's antics until, finally, the chill drove them back onto land. Here they dried themselves, using handfuls of the long, sweet-smelling prairie grass. Caleb was about to dress when Lone

14

Elk placed a restraining hand on his arm and wrinkled his nose. His next move took Caleb by surprise, for, snatching his clothing away from him, the Chief started back to the village.

'Hey, what the hell are you doing?' Caleb cried out. 'You can't leave me here naked.'

The Indian ignored his protest and so, running after him, Caleb managed to tug his woollen drawers free, putting them on quickly despite Lone Elk's obvious words of disapproval.

Conscious of his bare torso, Caleb hurried on ahead, though for all the notice the Mandans paid to him when he entered the village, he could have been fully dressed, coonskin hat as well.

'For the love of God, Zeb,' he protested to his now awake partner, 'tell him to give me my clothes back.'

The old trader grinned and shook his head. 'I'm just off to have a bathe myself, son, he replied. 'We're guests of his and I guess it's the least we can do. You and I must smell pretty high to these people, though you sure smell sweeter this morning.'

Chuckling to himself, he stripped down to his drawers then headed for the river. On Lone Elk's arrival, he said something to the women and the two older ones gathered up the clothing, using a wicker basket, placing Caleb's on top, before leaving the lodge. The girl busied herself about the cooking fire then brought two bowls of food over to where the men were seated. Her buckskin dress was unlaced to the waist, and when she leaned over, Caleb could see her breasts. She did not attempt to tighten the leather thongs, and, try as he might, he could not prevent his eyes straying to the moulded flesh. The girl noticed his gaze, on one occasion, yet simply smiled innocently back at him.

Later, in the company of Zeb and Lone Elk, he went down to the river to collect their trade goods.

'The Chief tells me that you fancy the young squaw, son,' Zeb said as they walked along. 'He says to tell you that she's yourn if she's willin',

Despite all his efforts to prevent it, Caleb felt his face warm in a blush.

'No such thing,' he spluttered, looking wildly about him. 'Ask him where he got that notion from?'

Zeb spoke briefly with the Chief then laughed loudly.

'He says to tell you that he's got eyes in his head. The girl is his daughter, Morning Star, and many of the tribal bucks desire her, though she won't have anything to do with them.'

Reaching their canoe, they found that everything was in its place, as Zeb had predicted and, with the help of a couple of passing warriors, they carried the goods into the centre of the village. In next to no time, the two traders were surrounded by both warriors and squaws, who inspected the iron goods with delight. Giving a demonstration, Zeb smashed a clay pot with one easy blow from a stick, but when its iron counter-part remained unmarked, the Indians cried out in wonder. Strangely enough, it was the three kettles in their display that took their customers' fancy and these soon changed hands for a goodly collection of furs.

'Darned if I know why these always go first,' Zeb remarked. 'Pity is, that's all I could git in Saint Louis. Reckon I'll have to build me a kettle factory someday.'

The bartering was brisk with little haggling from either side and Caleb noted that Zeb was more than fair in his dealings.

'Found it the best way to treat Indians,' his partner replied, when he commented on this. 'God willin', I'll be back here again some day and this tribe will be happy to see me.'

When the trading had ended, Zeb spoke with Lone Elk for a while, discussing the quality of the furs.

'Now these pelts are what I like the most,' he told the Chief, holding up some beaver skins, 'Save them for me, Lone Elk, and I will take all you have.'

The Indian stared hard at him for a moment, then spread his

arms wide, looking around him.

'We kill only to eat and clothe ourselves,' he said firmly. 'We do not kill our brothers of the earth for trade. Yet the beaver die as all of us do, and these we shall keep for you.'

Zeb thanked him and then helped Caleb tie their newly acquired furs into bundles.

'Jist had my knuckles rapped,' he told his partner. 'Serves me right, too. I should have known better. Most Injuns think of wild animals as their equals.'

Later that day, when the sun was lowering in the west, White Eagle visited the traders, to talk with Caleb. First of all, though, he spoke of the pleasure his people had experienced in their dealings with the white men.

'You have been generous and fair with them,' he told Zeb. 'You are welcome to visit us whenever you wish. Will you now help me to speak with your young friend?

Zeb thanked the Chief for his invitation to return to the village, then said that he would gladly translate

'Tell me of your homeland,' the Chief said, speaking directly to Caleb. 'Is it truly a country of great beauty?'

'According to my folks, it's the fairest land on earth,' Caleb answered. 'It has mountains, green valleys with rivers full of fish, and warm rains in the spring, to help the crops grow, and yet, the people have to pay dearly for this paradise. They even have to steal the fish, as they belong to a few powerful men.'

White Eagle frowned in bewilderment then slowly shook his head

'That cannot be,' he said softly. 'All things on Earth belong to the Great Spirit. Everyone knows that. Do you have buffalo in this Cymru, to feed and clothe yourselves?'

'No such luck,' Caleb answered, shaking his head. 'Ma used to say that many young uns would die every winter from cold and poor food.'

'Then it cannot be such a good place, my friend,' the Chief said sadly. 'It must be a land the Great Spirit has forgotten.'

He spoke on for a while longer, asking questions that Caleb could not fully answer, then made to take his leave.

'From what you say, I think my ancestors were right to come here, though many died making the journey over the big water.'

The two traders watched him walk away until he passed from their sight.

'What the hell did he mean by that?' Caleb asked, breaking the puzzled silence.

'Durned if I know,' Zeb answered, 'though I could have misunderstood him. Maybe big water could be a lake somewheres off. I guess we'll never know for sure.'

The following day, Zeb was persuaded to go hunting with Broken Lance. The big War Chief had a motive for the pressing invitation, one that he could not hide when the trader brought out his musket. The Indian's face lit up with pleasure and he clapped Zeb robustly on the shoulder.

'No doubting what he's after, Caleb,' the trader remarked. 'He ain't going to give me rest 'til he's fired the piece hisself.'

'Well, take care now, you hear,' Caleb replied. 'Keep well behind him. I don't want to make the trip back to Saint Louis on my own.'

He watched Zeb and the big Indian make their departure then, collecting his own musket, began to walk up the riverbank. For the first time in weeks, he was alone and revelling in the freedom as he moved leisurely through the long prairie grass. The day was already warm, the sky blue and the air heavy with the scent of wild flowers. He had walked more than a mile from the camp when he came to a stream, and this he followed to where it cut into a rise in the land. The ground here was overgrown with a tangle of bushes, so he began to climb around the obstruction, coming to a halt when he heard the sounds of voices. Peering over the undergrowth, he saw Morning Star in the company of two girls of her own age. She saw him at the same moment and called out his name, laughing as she did so.

Caleb heard her say something to her companions, who moved off, chuckling between themselves as they did so. Pushing her way through the bushes, Morning Star came up to where he stood and he saw that she carried a wicker basket, which was half-full of blueberries. She offered these to him and, taking a handful, he crammed the fruit into his mouth, savouring the sweet tasting juice. She spoke a few words in Lakotan to him but when Caleb did not reply, shrugged her shoulders as though it was of no matter. Instead, she caught hold of his sleeve and led him down to the stream. Nearing the water, she put the basket down; in one swift motion, she pulled her buckskin dress down to her ankles, and stepped clear. Caleb had a startled view of the naked girl standing before him for a moment, before Morning Star plunged into the stream. Turning onto her back, she motioned Caleb to join her. His first reaction was to run back to the camp but then, swallowing hard, he undressed and dived in. Laughing together, they swam for a while, occasionally standing in the shallower water to splash one another, until finally climbing out onto the bank. Here, they sat side by side and after a few moments, Caleb put his arm around the girl and drew her towards him. Morning Star's eyes opened wide as he placed his lips on hers; at first her body went rigid then suddenly she relaxed. When he made to draw back, she smiled with delight at him and returned the kiss.

The sun was well down in the west when the two left the place, walking hand in hand across the prairie. Their arrival at Lone Elk's lodge passed without comment, though Caleb felt eyes on him as he wolfed down his supper.

'You must have had a hard day, lad,' Zeb commented

dryly. 'Ye sure worked up an appetite, whatever it was ye was adoing.'

Caleb finished the last scrap of his meal, avoiding the trader's stare, and asked how the hunting had gone.

'It went well enough,' Zeb answered. 'Yet Broken Lance durned near blew my head off with his first shot. He insisted on waving the gun around as though it were some war lance. Got hisself a fine buck deer in the end, though.'

The pair spent three more idyllic days with the Mandans before making their departure. Whenever the opportunity arose, Caleb would go off with Morning Star; and it was with a great sadness that they spent their last few hours together. On the morning when he and Zeb finally pushed their canoe clear of the shingle beach, the whole village came to see them off. Caleb had scarcely paddled a stroke before Morning Star splashed through the swift, shallow water and flung her arms around him. The strength of the current, however, caused her to break her hold, and she stood forlornly in the river and raised a hand in farewell. She called his name and, as he looked back, she called once more, 'Caleb, CARIAD.'

The Missouri took the light craft in its grip and they were half a mile downstream before the word struck Caleb like a thunderbolt. He had often heard his mother say an endearment to his father in Welsh and the word she had used was '*cariad*', sweetheart. The feeling that these Mandans were different to other Indians became a certainty in his mind and he vowed that one day he would return.

2

1170 A.D.

Drawing his cloak closer about him, Madog braced himself against the fierce wind that came off the Irish Sea. The narrow pass along which he and his men were riding ran south-west and, therefore, caught the full force of the gale head on. With a word of encouragement and a tap of his heels, he urged his shaggy pony down the gentle slope, and the tough little animal responded immediately. Despite the difficult journey, his mount seemed to be still quite fresh, though Madog suspected that it was the thought of a warm stable and a pail of oats, which drove it on. Two miles further down, they came to an old, deeply rutted road and, without guidance, the pony turned to its left, causing a smile to lighten up its rider's face. Further along this road, the land opened up as the hills parted, and Madog looked eagerly over an expanse of flat marshland. Rising out of the watery ground, like an island in the sea, Moel-y-Gest stood before him, a natural fortress dominating the landscape.

'Almost home, Rhodri,' he called out, looking over his shoulder. 'We shall be seated by a warming fire shortly.'

The mailed figure riding some yards behind him raised his lance high for a moment and called back, though his words were snatched away by the wind. He, in turn, looked behind him, seeing the four spearmen and four bowmen sit more uprightly in their saddles at his gaze. Suppressing a grin, he gave them a wave of encouragement, and then looked ahead once more. Their mission, now almost completed, had been a peaceful one, yet in this year of our Lord, one thousand, one hundred and seventy, it was not wise to travel afar without an armed escort. Still, it kept men such as himself in employment, he mused.

A short distance further on, Madog came to an overgrown ruin and here his pony turned to its right without command. The ruin, as with the road, had been built hundreds of years ago by Roman legionaries, and he had been told that it had been used as a bathing place. These same men had also built the causeway along which he was now riding and, for the thousandth time, he marvelled at their skill. Their way now ran as straight as an arrow toward the steep northern face of Moel-y-Gest, and on finally reaching this, he skirted the high stone tower which guarded the exit. His father, to defend the only means of approach by land, had built the tower, and as usual, four of his retainers stood guard. They shouted out a welcome as he rode past, and he answered, calling each man by name, which he knew they found pleasing. His pony now turned left, following a well-worn track, which ran between the marsh and the hillside. Riding along this for more than a mile, Madog suddenly came to an estuary.

Drawing rein, he paused for some moments, taking in the vast expanse of space, which contrasted so sharply with the narrow mountain passes through which he had travelled. The tide was in and the water reflected the cold, blue, winter sky, making a picture of breathtaking beauty. Yet this beauty was deceptive, hiding dangerous shallows and sand banks, and God help anyone caught out there when the tide turned. The estuary filled and emptied at such speed that navigation became impossible. An ebb tide had swept Madog's father, mother, and two servants to their deaths in the previous autumn, despite their knowledge of the dangers. A sudden gust of wind had blown their craft from the relative safety of the Glaslyn river onto a submerged sandbank, turning the boat over. It had been ten days before the sea had finally given up their bodies, many miles down the coast, near Caryn Abbey.

Madog swallowed his grief then nudged the pony into a walk, and the animal almost immediately turned onto another track, which led up the gentle southern slope of Moel-y-Gest. A number of cottages stood close to the track, and as he and his escort rode past, several people called out a warm greeting to them. Their way now twisted and turned through thick woodland until, riding clear, they came to the shore of a small lake and before them stood Madog's home, Castell Morfa. His pony instantly broke into a bone-jarring trot, but, for once, its rider was happy to let it have its head. The gates of the wooden palisade were open, though guarded by two spearmen, who nimbly stepped aside as the riders passed. Only when it reached the stables did Madog's mount come to a stop, to peer over the closed lower half of the door.

Madog freed his booted feet from the stirrups, then gladly slid from the saddle, stamping his feet against the stiffness in his legs.

'Water and feed them well,' he told a servant who came running to meet them. 'Rest them on the morrow for they have had a hard ride today.'

He gave his mount an appreciative slap on its rump then began to walk across the yard, pausing to speak with Rhodri.

'Join me for supper when darkness falls,' he said to the thickset man-at-arms. 'I think that we have much to discuss.'

'That I will, sire, and gladly,' Rhodri replied. 'I ate little this morning and my belly is rumbling in protest.'

Madog continued across the yard, to find an old man waiting for him in the doorway that led into the great stone and timbered hall.

'Welcome back, sire. I trust your journey was successful,' the elder said.

'Only in part, Cynon,' Madog told him, loosening his cloak. 'I met with the Prince and renewed my father's oath of allegiance

23

to him. I was then received with the best of hospitality by his court. However, all is not well. Owain Gwynedd is in poor health and is plagued by his brother, who desires to seize power.'

Cynon moved aside and Madog strode into the lofty room, making for the hearth in which a cheering fire gave out its warmth. Throwing his cloak over a nearby bench, he nudged with his foot the two wolfhounds that lay in front of the fire and, reluctantly, the animals moved aside. Thankfully, he crouched down in the small space they had made for him and, for a few moments, he enjoyed the enveloping heat.

'Here, sire, drink this,' Cynon said, offering him a goblet. 'It will warm you from your inside.'

Madog took the proffered goblet and looked at the clear liquid that it contained, before raising it to his lips. The Water of Life slid down his throat and he felt a warm glow spread through his innards.

'My thanks, Cynon,' he gasped, handing the now empty goblet back. 'Be sure to give my escort a drink each when they come to eat, and save some for Rhodri. You know how much he appreciates the drink.'

'Indeed I do, sire. Indeed I do,' the elder muttered disapprovingly, stroking his grey moustache. 'His liking for heady drinks is well known on Moel-y-Gest.'

Madog chuckled to himself as he stood up and slung his cloak over his shoulder. Rhodri's boisterous lifestyle often offended his steward's sense of decorum, though the old man tried hard to keep this to himself. The man-at-arms was so skilled in the art of war, that this far outweighed his coarse manner.

Leaving the warmth of the hearth, he crossed the hall, skirting the massive table, which ran half the length of the room, and climbed an open stairway. At the top, he followed a balcony, passing one of the bedchambers that had been used by his parents. As always, he felt the grief and emptiness within him as he saw the closed door. The tragedy had happened almost four months ago, yet his sense of loss was as deep as on the day of the event. The adjoining chamber was his and he entered, pleased to see that a small fire glowed in the open hearth. A stack of logs lay to one side and he placed several of these on the embers, blowing gently until the wood began to burn. He then stripped off his soiled clothing, washed himself in a basin of cold water, then dressed in a clean shirt and tunic. There was still light coming through the open shutter of the narrow window, so he closed it before lying down on the bed, his mind turning over his visit to the Prince's court. Owain's welcome had indeed been a warm one, though touched with sympathy for his young visitor.

'Your father and I were friends for many years,' Owain had told him. 'He was one of my staunchest supporters and always offered his sword, whenever I had need of it. Rest assured that you shall have the protection of my house, as did he.'

Madog gave a weary sigh and closed his eyes. He was not yet eighteen years of age and he found the responsibilities so tragically thrust upon him hard to cope with. He awoke with a start, to hear the sounds of laughter coming from below. Rubbing the sleep from his eyes, he swung himself up from the bed and swiftly left the chamber. Downstairs, he found that the men who had made up his escort were already eating, in the company of several others. They greeted him as he passed the table, wishing him good health with raised tankards. At the end of the hall, he came to a door and, opening this, he entered a smaller room, where Rhodri and Cynon sat waiting for him. He motioned them to remain seated, as they began to rise, and sat down himself at the well-worn table. The steward filled a tankard with ale from a jug and handed it to him before calling to a man servant who waited in the hall. The man shortly entered, carrying bowls of hot food, which the three began to eat. They ate in silence at first, until Cynon judged that the others had appeased their hunger.

'Tell me more of your meeting with Prince Owain, sire,' he said. 'Is he truly a sickly man?'

'Indeed he is,' Madog answered, between mouthfuls of stew. 'There is still fire in his eyes when he speaks of his enemies, yet his body is frail. The strength of the great warrior, which he once was, has gone from him and I fear he will not regain it.' Cynon's brow creased into a frown and he fell silent for a while, stirring his food absentmindedly.

'Your words both sadden and concern me,' he eventually remarked. 'We have known years of peace here on Moel-y-Gest, under his protection. What news is there of his brother, Cadwaladr? Did you see him at the court?'

'He was not present during my stay, though his sons were,' Madog answered. 'I do not know which of the two I disliked the most. They strutted around as though their father already ruled. Owain's steward told me in confidence that several of the Prince's supporters had already fled his court, fearing for their lives and property.'

'Then, we had best be on our guard,' Cynon advised. 'Your father had nothing but contempt for Cadwaladr and his ambitions, and that villain knew it well. He is not a man to forget or forgive such feelings. It would be wise, sire, to send a man back to the court, to keep watch on events.'

Madog thought this over for a few moments and saw the sense in his steward's advice,

'What you say seems wise,' he said. 'Choose someone of ability and send him on the morrow.'

He saw Rhodri reach over for the ale jug and refill his tankard, the candlelight showing up his dark features. As with most Welshmen, the man-at-arms kept his face shaven, and the light emphasised the white scars he had earned in combat.

'What do you honestly think of our chances of holding Moel-

26

y-Gest, were we to be attacked?' Madog asked him.

Rhodri drank deeply, then set his tankard down on the table.

'It would depend on the numbers that opposed us, sire,' he answered. 'Counting yourself, we have but eighteen fighting men. Then there are the five tenant farmers and some ten fishermen who all know how to handle a spear or sword. Between us, we could hold the causeway easily enough. Where our weakness lies is an attack from the sea.' He paused for a moment, then gave a wicked grin. 'Of course, you could ask that blonde giant and his men down on the beach to aid us.'

'The Norseman is but passing through,' Madog replied. 'He could be gone by next month. He is anxious to finish his repairs and sail to Ireland, where he can replace the men he lost in the storm.'

'A pity, sire,' Rhodri said. 'Men such as he can be worth a score of others in a fight.'

The man-at-arms refilled his tankard, and Madog guessed that he would continue to do so until he fell asleep. The young man did not intend to get involved in a drinking bout; at that moment, he wanted to be able to think clearly. Bidding his companions sleep well, he left them and walked through the hall, where most of his men now lay on straw pallets set against one wall. Once inside his chamber, he said a prayer, quickly undressed, then slid into bed. His prayer had been for a continued peace here at Castell Morfa, yet the unease that he had felt at Owain's court still hung over him. The memory of the cold stares Cadwaladr's sons had directed at him remained clear in his mind and he had been glad to have Rhodri at his side. There was no chieftain in the north strong enough to oppose the Prince's brother, and Madog suddenly felt very lonely and vulnerable.

He awoke in the morning from a restless sleep. Washing and dressing himself, he went down the stairs and entered the kitchen, where the warm smell of baking bread greeted him. A jug of milk stood on a ledge, and, filling a bowl with the liquid, Madog drank slowly, only half hearing the chatter of the women servants busy about him. Badly in need of fresh air to clear his fuddled head, he fastened his cloak tightly and stepped outside, only to find that the wind had dropped. Although it was February, the day felt almost balmy, and, with a light step, he crossed the yard and passed through the gateway. He followed the track leading to the cottages for a short distance, then turned right down a path that twisted its way through the trees, eventually coming to a sandy cove. Several of the trees close by had been recently felled, and Madog saw some fair-headed men sawing away at lengths of timber. From further along the cove, there came the sounds of hammering, and he began to trudge through the sand toward the noise, passing a rock outcrop, which stood as though on guard against the sea. Only then could he see the large boat, which had been drawn up the beach, and now lay above the high-tide mark. Many years ago, the sight of such a craft would have struck terror into the people of Moel-y-Gest, as it signalled the approach of the feared Vikings. These days, however, the men from the distant north preferred to trade peacefully, rather than pillage. This particular boat, though, was not built for commerce; its high prow and stern and its long, slender lines spoke of speed through the water. Superbly designed and built for this purpose, the boat's beauty was marred by a wide gash in its side, which was why it now lay like a beached whale in the sand. Stepping over the stout mast, which lay clear of the activity, and avoiding the carefully folded sail, Madog approached the men working on the boat.

'Good day to you, Eric,' he called out. 'I trust your task proceeds well?'

From amongst the men, a huge figure put down his hammer and walked towards him.

'Not as well as I had hoped,' he answered, in broken Welsh. 'We have much trouble in finding the right timber. Your oaks in these parts are too small, and of pine you have very few. This makes our work hard to do and calls for patience. It will take longer than I had first thought.'

He grasped Madog's forearm in greeting and looked down at the young man, his long, blonde hair falling over his shoulders.

'I hope you will suffer our presence here for a while,' he said.

'There is no urgency for you to leave,' Madog told him. 'You are welcome to stay as long as you like. My people are happy enough at your being here, for you pay them well enough for your food.'

He ran a critical eye over the damaged craft, seeing that progress had, indeed, been slow, yet that which had been done was excellent in its quality.

'It is a miracle that any of you survived that storm,' he said. 'God must have shown pity that day.'

'Your God and ours,' Eric replied. 'It was the worst storm that I have known in all the years that I have sailed the seas. We lost half our number in one great wave. All we could do was to hold on tightly to the rowing benches and pray.'

'Will you still go in search of your new world, after such a terrible disaster?' Madog asked.

'Indeed, I will,' Eric answered fervently, his blue eyes coming alive. 'I shall sail to Ireland and find more oarsmen. There are many Norsemen living there these days. There is a new world out there, you know; our ancestors found it a long while ago.' He stared off into the western sky and, seeing the emotion on the big man's face, Madog felt sure that, if anyone could succeed in such an adventure, it would be Eric.

Taking his leave, he began to retrace his steps along the

beach, his mind forming into a daydream in which he joined the Norseman on his journey into the unknown. There was little chance of that, though, he told himself. His duty lay with the people of Moel-y-Gest, and ensuring that Castell Morfa prospered. Eric watched the young man walk away and felt a surge of affection course through him. He had traded along the Welsh coast for years, yet had never formed a true friendship with any of these proud, independent people. Yet, he had taken a great liking to Madog, at the moment of their first meeting. On impulse, he ran after the Welshman and laid a restraining hand on his shoulder,

'I want you to know that I am truly thankful for your help and hospitality,' he said. 'I shall always be in your debt.'

Madog smiled up at him, then shrugged his shoulders.

'You were in need of aid and it was mine to give,' he replied. 'Now get back to your boat, my friend, and think about that new world of yours.'

On his return to Castell Morfa, he found Cynon speaking with a short, slim man, who was getting on in years. The man, who was named Iorwerth, was well known to Madog, having visited the Castell on many occasions, to entertain the people with songs and poems. The steward broke off his conversation at Madog's approach,

'I have asked Iorwerth to travel to Owain's court and act as our eyes and ears, sire,' Cynon told him. 'He has agreed to do so, if we will provide him with a pony.'

'You shall have the sturdiest mount in my stable, Iorwerth,' Madog enthused. 'I can think of no-one better suited for this task than you. There are always bards visiting the court, so you will not attract any special attention. You are still in good voice, I trust?'

Iorwerth's intelligent, dark eyes twinkled with amusement at the question.

'That I am, sire, though there are some of us who could not tell whether I sang, or groaned.'

Madog winced visibly at his jibe. It was well known that he could not tell one note from another, which made him something of an oddity amongst a people who loved music.

'Yes, well, I must take your word then,' he stammered. 'Tell no-one that you are from Moel-y-Gest, but you are simply another travelling bard. Should anything happen to Owain, return here as quickly as possible and let Cynon or myself know.'

He chose a reliable pony from the stable and helped Iorwerth to harness and mount the animal.

'Take care, now,' he warned the bard, handing him his harp. 'Remember that we have enemies as well as friends at the Prince's court. Keep your own council and all should be well with you.'

The little musician nodded his understanding and, with a brief wave, rode through the gates. Standing in the opening, Madog watched him ride alongside the lake, until pony and rider passed from his sight amongst the trees. Silently praying that when he next saw Iorwerth it would be to receive good news, he turned back into the yard and headed for the kitchen.

3

The days passed by and Madog slipped back into the routine of supervising life on Moel-y-Gest. His mornings were spent either with one of the farm tenants, or amongst the fishermen, sometimes going to sea with one of the latter, to fish in the bay. The matter of Prince Owain's health gradually faded to the back of his mind, as he attended to other problems closer to hand; Rhodri brought it back to the fore, one sunny afternoon. It was on a day when Eric had paid him a rare visit at Castell Morfa. The Norseman had asked permission to search further inland for timber, to which Madog had agreed, and the two were standing in the gateway when Rhodri and his four bowmen walked past.

'We are going to practice archery, sire,' the man-at-arms said. 'Perhaps it would be wise were you to join us. It takes many months to become proficient with our Welsh bows, though it would be useful were you to learn the basic skills. Elise here would be happy to teach you.'

Madog looked at the tall, lithe bowman, who gave him a wide grin.

'It would be my pleasure, sire,' he said, 'though I have yet to meet one of you northerners who can master the bow. You seem to lack the patience needed. You have the height and seem strong enough to handle the weapon.'

Elise and his comrades came from along the banks of the River Usk, which ran its course many miles away, in southeast Wales. The men from those parts were famed throughout the land for their skill with the longbow, and were in great demand to serve under the banners of Welsh chieftains. Such was the demand that the bowmen asked for payment in coin, which was why Madog had only four in his retinue. Nodding his agreement, he was about to bid Eric farewell when the Norseman, surprisingly, expressed his wish to accompany them. Elise seemed to be taken aback by this and looked enquiringly at Rhodri.

'Do as he asks,' the man-at-arms told him. 'Look on the Norseman as a friend, as your employer does.'

To the north of the Castell lay a fine stretch of meadowland, it was to here that the group made their way, stopping some hundred paces from two straw-filled dummy figures. Here the bowmen strung their six-feet-long staffs, notched an arrow, then, drawing back on the string, loosed at the targets. Of the four, only one struck home, yet, within moments, they had loosed again, repeating this until each man had shot six arrows. When the bowmen finally lowered their staffs, the targets had more than ten goose-feathered shafts protruding from them. Walking across the meadow with Elise, to retrieve the arrows, Madog found that the shafts had pierced the straw dummies, only the flights showing at the front.

'You must not draw back too far on your bow string, sire,' Elise told him, when Madog remarked on this. 'Should you do so, the arrow will pass through, so that you could not tell whether or not you have struck the target. You will find this out for yourself, when you try out the bow.'

His words were true enough, as Madog found out when, later, he drew back on the bowstring. The strength of the staff surprised him, for though he only drew until he felt the first pressure, his released arrow sped some seventy paces before hitting the ground. On his second attempt, he drew back until his arms began to quiver under the strain and, when he loosed, the arrow flew past its target, to land more than fifty paces beyond. Under Elise's coaching, he eventually began to drop his arrows closer to the dummy, until at last, one of them struck home.

His upper arms and chest were aching in protest by now and, with a sense of relief, he handed the bow back to his tutor. 'That is enough for the present,' he said. 'I thank you for the lesson. Show me how far you can shoot, Elise.'

The bowman notched an arrow, shifted his feet until his left leg was well in front of the other, and then drew back, raising the bow in the same motion. Without pausing, he released the string and Madog had a glimpse of the arrow as it shot into the sky. For a few moments, he lost sight of it and then, far down the meadow, he saw a white blob streak to earth.

'That must be three hundred paces, at least,' he exclaimed in astonishment. 'Can your comrades match that?'

'Indeed they can, sire,' Elise answered. 'We can do an enemy much hurt, long before he can get close to us. Ask the English Marcher knights. They have felt our sting more than most, and have come to respect our skill. You should practice every day, sire, for I believe that you have the knack.' He smiled broadly and gestured to where Eric was standing with one of the other bowmen.

'As you can see, sire, it takes more than brute strength to handle a longbow.' Looking toward the Norseman, Madog saw the big man toss a bow back to its owner. There were no arrows to be seen anywhere near Eric's target, and his face showed his frustration.

'Hell and damnation,' he snorted. 'That is no way for a man to fight in battle. Should the Gods give him the strength, then, he must use it and smash his foe to pieces. I will keep my trust in my axe. It has served me well enough, whenever I've had need of it.'

The two left the bowmen at their archery and made their way to the head of the path that led down to the cove. Here, they parted company, the young nobleman promising to visit Eric on the morrow. Eventful as the day had been, there was still more to come, for as Madog sat down to his supper, there was a commotion in the hall. The door of his private chamber suddenly burst open without ceremony to admit the dishevelled figure of Iorwerth. For a moment or two, the little bard swayed in the doorway, then, as Madog and Rhodri sprang to his assistance, he staggered into the room. Between them, the two helped him into a chair by the hearth, while Cynon hurriedly poured him a drink of the Water of Life. Containing his impatience, Madog waited until the bard had drunk the last drop of the spirit, and then knelt beside him.

'It can only be bad news that brings you home in such haste,' he said. 'Has Prince Owain's health worsened?'

Iorwerth shook his head and looked appealingly at Cynon, who poured him another drink.

'I fear my news is even more alarming, sire,' he gasped. 'The Prince is dead and his brother, Cadwaladr, has seized power. A few of the chieftains were bold enough to oppose him and were slain in cold blood. Before fleeing the court, I learned that Cadwaladr has placed his two sons in command of his army.'

Madog felt himself turn cold at this news and poured himself a mouthful of spirit.

'Did you see their army?' he asked.

'Yes, sire,' Iorwerth answered. 'They marched in and camped close to the court. They number almost one thousand men, by my counting.'

Despite every effort to remain calm, Madog felt his hand begin to shake, and he hastily placed his goblet down on the table. One thousand men against his thirty-three. What hope did he have of holding Moel-y-Gest? Even Rhodri seemed stunned, staring glumly at the floor.

'You must be mistaken, Iorwerth,' the man-at-arms said eventually. 'No chieftain in Wales commands such numbers.'

''Tis as true as I'm sitting here,' the bard retorted. 'Cadwaladr had his sons march their men past Owain's people, to show his strength. Many of them are from Powys and eager for booty.'

He fell silent for a while, avoiding the eyes of his companions, then, giving a deep sigh, he spoke on.

'There is worse, I'm afraid, sire,' he said. 'Cadwaladr has proclaimed that those who supported Prince Owain must forfeit their lands, or be put to the sword. He says that he must take this step to prevent any treacherous act against him.'

'Then, he does not leave a man a choice,' Madog burst out angrily. 'One thousand men or more, he will have to fight for Moel-y-Gest.'

The others sat in silence, each man willing the other two to say something. It was Rhodri who finally did so, shifting uncomfortably in his chair.

'Speaking for myself and my men, you can rely on us to fight, sire,' he said. 'That is what we are paid to do. Yet I think it madness to face such odds, even though we have the causeway. However, if it is your command, so be it.'

'What of the women and children and the elderly?' Cynon asked. 'There are more than one hundred souls on this island, and it is your duty to think of everyone's safety.'

Madog got to his feet and began to pace up and down the room, his mind in turmoil. His sudden outburst had surprised him as much as the others, yet he could not stomach the thought of Cadwaladr or his sons tramping through Castell Morfa, but he could not condemn Rhodri and his men to a certain death, or leave his people to the dubious mercy of the new Prince. He had almost despaired of finding an answer when a thought struck him, bringing him to a halt. Either he could die in battle, be a pauper and unwilling servant, or he could leave Moel-y-Gest. Painful though it was, the last option was preferable to the other two. Yet, where were they to go and how? With children and the elderly, any progress overland would be slow, and he did not know if a route to the south would still be open to him. It had to be the sea which offered the best chance of escape. They could sail until they found a friendly shore, where they could start life again.

'How many of our people could we safely embark in our fishing boats?' he asked of no-one in particular.

'No more than fifty-five, at a guess,' Cynon answered, after a pause. 'What do you have in mind, sire? I must confess, I am bewildered by your question.'

''Tis clear enough, old friend,' Madog answered bitterly. 'We can stay here and live like slaves, or leave and be free men. I know which I prefer, and feel sure that the men of Moel-y-Gest will think likewise. When morning comes, summon them to attend me here. They must make up their own minds on a matter as grave as this.' 'What if everyone chooses to leave?' Rhodri asked. 'You cannot offer them all a place in the boats, and it would be unjust to leave some behind.'

'I shall buy a boat large enough to take the remainder,' Madog answered. 'I have monies enough for this, I believe.'

He looked at Cynon, who nodded in agreement, then he added, 'You will see to this for me. We shall see what the people wish to do, first, then, if needs be, you can sail to the Mawddach with men to crew the boat you purchase. The men of those parts have a reputation for building stout craft, and we have always been on friendly terms with them.'

The old man slumped in his chair and held his head in both hands, then raised a tearful face.

'I shall do as you say, sire,' he choked out, 'though it will be with a heavy heart. My life has been spent on Moel-y-Gest, and the thought of leaving fills me with sorrow.'

Madog walked over to the table and placed his hands on the old man's shoulders.

'You are not alone in your grief, Cynon,' he said gently,

'but I have no choice. You may stay, if you wish, and have my blessing.'

Cynon shook his head and grasped Madog's hands in his.

'I shall serve you as I did your father and his father,' he said, 'no matter where that may be.'

Madog was taking his leave when Rhodri spoke on another matter.

'It would be wise to send a small patrol up to the top of the pass,' he said. 'They can give us an early warning, should our foe move against us.'

Madog gave his assent, then, after bidding the others to sleep well, he made his way up to his chamber.

The sun was already low in the sky, on the following day, when he made his way down to the cove. After a restless night, he had spent the morning inspecting his armoury with Rhodri, who had expressed his satisfaction at the condition of the various weapons.

The man-at-arms had then picked four of his men and, placing himself at their head, had ridden for the pass, leaving Madog to meet with his tenants. The fishermen and farmers had listened silently at first to his news of Cadwaladr's edict, then, with a growing anger as he explained its meaning to them.

'My father always treated you as his equals, which our old laws demanded he should do. He asked little of you except your loyalty and a token rent for your homes and lands. All this will change under Cadwaladr, as we are not strong enough to prevent it. Rather than live here under such conditions, I am leaving Moel-y-Gest and shall go in search of a new home. Should it be your wish, any man here is welcome to join me.'

He then told them of his plan and answered their many questions as best he could. Only one of these did he leave unanswered and that was whither they would sail.

'I do not know,' he told them frankly. 'We must place our faith in God and trust that he will guide us to a friendly shore.'

The men had talked amongst themselves at great length and then, to his gratification, had decided unanimously to leave with him if attacked.

Reaching the beach, he trudged wearily through the sand and halted when he had passed the rock outcrop. The incoming tide was now flowing swiftly up river and before him, lying proudly at anchor, was Eric's craft. He and his men were gathered around its prow, and the big Norseman called out, inviting Madog to join them. Firstly kicking off his soft, leather boots, the young man waded into the water, its coldness gripping his bare feet.

'Come and see what Bjorn has carved for me,' Eric cried out excitedly, making room for him. 'He has been whittling away every night by firelight.'

Madog stepped into the empty space and saw that a carving of a large wolf's head now adorned the boat's bow. Though the workmanship was somewhat crude, there was no mistaking what it portrayed. With lips drawn back in a snarl, exposing teeth and fangs, the head was a frightening object to behold.

'This replaces the one we lost in the storm,' Eric told him. 'My forefathers have always followed the wolf's head when at sea. It always brought them good fortune in the days when they went raiding.'

'But, why is the boat afloat?' Madog asked. I understood that you had more work to do before it was safe for you to sail.'

'Two more days, my friend, will see the repairs finished,' Eric said. 'We found a good size tree inland, which will make our work much easier. We have floated our boat to make the timbers swell, which keeps the water from seeping in.'

They waded ashore together and, after drying their feet in the sand, sat down to put their boots on. Eric gave the young

Welshman a searching look when he stood up.

'What troubles you, Madog?' he asked. 'You look as though you had no rest last night, and your manner is not as usual.'

Before he could stop himself, Madog was pouring out his troubles to the big man.

'My people are going to have to leave here,' he said. 'I am convinced that Cadwaladr will make a move against Moel-y-Gest as soon as he can. He hated my father for being such a staunch friend to Prince Owain. I have told my steward to take some of our men and buy a boat large enough to hold some fifty people. With that and the fishing boats, everyone will have the chance to flee.'

Eric towered above him, his brow creased in thought.

'I shall help you, Madog,' he said suddenly. 'You may have need of all your fighting men. Give me two days and I will take your steward to wherever he wishes. We are short of oarsmen, yet we can still handle our boat. Let me do this, my friend,' he added, as Madog began to protest. 'It is my wish to repay you for your hospitality. 'Madog thanked him, and then took his leave. In the growing gloom of evening, he made his way back to Castell Morfa, where he ate supper and, shortly afterwards, retired to his bed. To his surprise, Cynon had seemed content enough to sail with the Norsemen on his mission.

'I believe you have found a true friend in that foreigner, sire,' he had said. ''Tis strange, I know, but I am happy to place myself and your money in his hands.'

As he lay in his bed, Madog thought about his steward's remark. Oddly enough, his troubles seemed to have lightened since his talk with Eric, and with this in his mind, he slipped into a deep sleep.

4

His mind on other matters, Madog allowed his pony to make its own way along the track leading to the causeway. The previous day, he had waved farewell to Eric and his men as their boat moved carefully down to the sea on an ebb tide. He still had a vivid memory of Cynon standing in the stern, returning his wave, somehow cutting a lonely figure amongst the Norsemen. Despite the gaps along the shield battens, the high-prowed craft slid easily downstream, its wolf's head seeming eager to reach open water. Scrambling along the rock outcrop, Madog had watched the boat eventually clear the estuary and turn south, its raised black and orange sail filling from a northerly wind. He had stayed on the rock until the boat disappeared behind a headland, then praying for its swift return, he had made his way homeward along the now deserted cove.

This morning, he was riding to the causeway in answer to a summons from Rhodri. The man-at-arms had returned to Castell Morfa, after positioning his men in the pass, then, after consuming a hurried meal and a jug of ale, he had ridden back to the causeway. Madog had not seen him since then and was growing worried about the mercenary's absence, when the messenger had arrived. Casting aside all thoughts of yesterday, Madog tapped his mount's flanks with his booted feet, and in answer, the pony began to walk faster. They had turned away from the estuary, and as they followed the track, Madog's eyes followed the line of hills opposite. Apart from a diminutive flock of sheep and a shepherd half way up, the slopes and crests were empty of life. The emptiness gave Madog some comfort, though he knew that the danger, when it came, would be from the pass, and he turned his eyes back to the rough track.

Ahead of him, the tower came into sight, and as he rode closer, he could make out some men, who were standing waist deep in the marsh beside the causeway. One of the men had a long, iron pole, and Madog could see that he was using it to prise loose one of the packed stones. Levering it free, he picked it up and, with an effort, passed it to the man next to him, who struggled to dry land before dropping the heavy object.

'Welcome, sire,' the mud-stained figure called out, his teeth showing white against the grime. 'My thanks for coming here so promptly. I have taken it upon myself to make a start on my idea. I hope you will approve. It makes sense to destroy as much of the causeway as we can and so deny our enemy an easy approach.'

Madog slid off the pony's back and walked over to the marsh edge. A gap of roughly one yard in length had been made where the causeway joined dry land, though he could see that it only reached water level.

'I know little about road-building, sire,' Rhodri said, his eyes following Madog's scrutiny. 'Yet this causeway was built to last. It is proving to be more difficult than I'd first thought. Four of us made a start at daybreak and, as you can see, we have little to show for our efforts.'

'Your idea is a good one, though it is plain that you need more help,' Madog told him. 'It will be best if I summon the men myself. I can convince them that this task is of great urgency, should anyone think differently. Have you had any word from your men at the pass?'

'None, sire,' Rhodri answered, shaking his head. 'I left them with enough food for five days and shall be relieving them on the morrow. Yet, I feel that all is not well, for there have been no travellers on yonder road today.'

Madog looked across the marsh in the direction of the ruined bathhouse. Rough though it was, the old road was by far the easiest route from the Lleyn Peninsula to much of the country, and it was strange not to see someone moving along it.

'No doubt people have heard rumours of Cadwaladr's plans,' he said. 'Only a fool would risk meeting up with his soldiers. Besides which, a man always feels safer when he is close to home.'

Mounting his pony, he took one more look around him.

'Persevere with your work, Rhodri. I shall get help to you as swiftly as I can.'

He found the fishermen working on their boats, which lay in a line on the beach. They listened attentively as he told them of Rhodri's plan and, to a man, agreed to go and help.

'You will need tools of some kind to move the stones,' Madog told them. 'They are using an iron bar. Have you anything suitable?'

The fishermen thought for a moment, until one of them, a man named Maredudd, smote his brow.

'What better than an anchor and a length of rope!' he cried. 'We all have one of these and they should be strong enough for the task. Would you tell Owain what we are about, sire?' he asked. 'He may think something is amiss when he sees us leave.'

'That I will,' Madog assured him. 'Now, make haste, my friends. The greater the gap in the causeway, the greater our chances of survival.'

He waited until the fishermen set off, then urged his pony forward and rode along the wet sands towards the estuary mouth. Similar to the opposite shore, a low headland marked the beginning of the sea, and, on reaching this, Madog dismounted and led his mount up a steep path. Reaching the top, he saw a pony cropping the short, winter grass, while its owner stood atop a hillock, looking up the estuary.

'Are we being attacked, Madog?' Owain asked excitedly. 'I saw you speak with the others and watched them leave in some haste. By the saints, I was sure Cadwaladr could not reach us until the morrow.'

'Rest easy, Owain,' Madog replied. ''Tis simply that their muscle is needed at the causeway.'

He went on to tell the young man of Rhodri's plan and of the difficulties the task presented.

'I shall be riding around the holdings, to get the farmers' help, also,' he added. Owain was some eight months older than Madog, and as children, they had played together around Castell Morfa. Their friendship had strengthened through the years and, whenever they were together, they spoke as equals. Madog studied the other man's handsome, weathered, tanned face for a few moments, then, on impulse, spoke on.

'What do you really think of our chances to escape and find a new life?' he asked bluntly.

Owain looked out over the sea, his eyes fixing on some fishing boats about two miles away. The boats seemed so small and frail against the immensity of the sea, he thought.

'Our escape will be in the hands of God and the temper of the sea,' he answered. 'Should the weather be fair, then we can succeed, but were there to be a storm, who knows what would happen. As for a new life, Madog, that is quite another matter. Were I a Norseman, I would follow that blonde giant in pursuit of his dreams, but then, my loyalty is to you.'

Deeply touched by Owain's last words, and not trusting himself to speak further, Madog merely nodded before leading his pony back down the path. For the hundredth time since his father's death, he cursed his responsibilities, and prayed that the loyalty of Owain and the others was not misplaced.

It was well past noon when he rode into Castell Morfa. Unsaddling the pony, he made sure that there was hay and water in its stable, and then made his way to the kitchen. Here, he made himself a meal of bread and cold meat and sat on one of the benches to eat it. The two women could see that he was in no mood for conversation, and left him with his thoughts, talking quietly to each other while preparing food. Except for one man, the farmers had readily agreed to stop work and go to Rhodri's aid. The dissenter, though, had refused to have any hand in defending the island.

'I've changed my mind, sire,' he had said. 'You are asking me to give up all I own and risk my life on some mad plan of escape. I have decided to take my chances with the new Prince. After all, I've never done him harm.'

Madog had not argued with the man, and had left him at his work, though telling him that a place on one of the boats would be kept for him and his family.

His repast completed, he climbed up to the gallery, stopping at his parent's chamber. Going in, he crossed the room to where a colourful tapestry covered part of one wall and drew it aside. In a deep niche, his father's chain-mail shirt hung on a wooden pole, surmounted by a head-ring of beaten silver, which held a ruby in its centre. Almost reverently, he took them down and slipped the shirt over his head. The metal linked garment fell below his hips and hung loosely around his shoulders, yet it offered protection against a sword's edge. His father's sword stood propped against a side of the niche, and Madog buckled this around his waist, before pulling the hood of the shirt over his head. With both hands, he placed the silver ring over this, and discovered that the metal band fitted snugly over his brow. Had he been able to see his reflection, he would have been surprised by the transformation. The youthful, almost boyish, Lord of Moel-y-Gest was gone, to be replaced by a warrior. Before leaving, Madog took one last look around the room, until his eyes came to rest on his parents' bed. Clasping his hands to his heart, he prayed that they would understand and agree with his decision to leave. He closed the door softly behind him, and then

45

went down the stairway and walked over to the stable. His pony nickered a greeting and came readily out into the yard, where Madog tightened its girth before mounting. The weight of the chain mail and sword hampered his movement, causing the pony to skitter sideways at his clumsiness. He leaned forward until his mouth almost touched one of its ears and spoke soothingly to the animal. After a few moments, his mount calmed down and obeyed its rider's command to walk on. Madog nodded to the lonely sentry at the gate as he rode past, and the man raised his spear in salute.

'You will not forget that I'm here, sire,' he called out.

'I will not; be sure of that,' Madog called back. 'Rest assured, you will be summoned when needed.'

On the road to the causeway, he overtook several women who were carrying baskets of food. He had passed them by when he suddenly drew rein and trotted back to them.

'A good day to you,' he said. 'My thanks for your thoughtfulness. Your men folk will be more than pleased to see you, of that I'm sure.'

The women put down their baskets and eyed the chain-mail shirt.

'By the Saints, you look like your father, sire!' one of them exclaimed. 'Indeed, when you rode past, I thought my eyes were playing tricks on me.'

Madog smiled at her but let the comment pass.

'When your task at the causeway had been done, I want one of you to perform another kindness,' he said. 'Owain, the fisherman, is alone on the headland, keeping watch, and he must be getting hungry by now.'

'I shall see to it, sire, and gladly,' the youngest of the women said, speaking quickly. The others chuckled amongst themselves, while Madog looked at the speaker. Tall and slender, with long, dark brown hair, and her complexion deepening in a blush, the girl was a beauty. In their childhood, she had often played with Owain and Madog, whenever they were willing to accept a member of the opposite sex into their games. It was no secret that the girl now adored the young fisherman, though no-one knew for sure what his feelings were.

'Thank you, Helen,' Madog replied, managing to keep a serious expression on his face. 'I'm sure Owain will be glad of your attention.'

Raising a hand in salute, he wheeled the pony around and rode on. Although he had not uttered a word in reply, the woman's remark about his appearance had filled him with pride. While only taking up his sword as a last resort, his father had had a reputation as a skilful and fearless leader in battle. As with all young Welshmen, Madog had been trained in the art of war, yet he wondered how he would react to the dangers encountered in conflict. His arrival at the causeway was scarcely noticed, so busily engaged were the men, though Rhodri paused long enough to speak a few words.

'Your mission has proved a success, as you can see, sire,' he said. 'The arrival of the fishermen and farmers has made a great impact already.'

Madog could see that some ten yards of stonework had been removed and that the men were now working on the foundations, which lay under water. He was about to remove the silver ring from his head when the man-at-arms stayed the movement.

'There is no call for you to join the others, sire,' he said. 'We are enough for the task and you are our commander.' He slid back into the mire, and then looked up at the young man. 'I must say that you look the part, sire,' he added approvingly.

Not prepared to stand idly on the bank, Madog was about to go to the tower when a movement at the far end of the causeway caught his eye. Four horsemen had begun to ride in single file along the roadway, and their number told him who they were.

'Your scouts are returning, Rhodri,' he called out, trying to keep his voice even.

The man-at-arms looked up sharply and, seeing the riders, squelched through the muddy water towards them. Reaching the demolished end of their road, the horsemen drew rein, dismounting as Rhodri spoke with them. Carefully, they led their mounts down the broken stonework into the water, and then made for firm ground.

'The men have sighted our foe, sire,' Rhodri gasped as he heaved himself up onto the bank. 'It was impossible for them to take a count, due to the turns in the pass, though all four reckon they saw more than five hundred, before they had to leave their post.'

Madog became aware that all eyes were now glued on him, and he forced himself to remain calm.

'Get the men onto dry land and tell them to clean themselves,' he ordered Rhodri. 'There is food on its way, and when they have eaten, tell them to go home and rest. At daybreak, they must meet you at the armoury, to collect their weapons, then you will lead them back here. Our foe will not reach here before darkness falls, so we shall be safe for tonight. I shall stay here with the four bowmen.'

Rhodri's face showed his agreement and, the next moment, he was repeating the commands in a loud voice, for all to hear.

Later, with the sun already down in the sky, Madog stood atop the tower in company with Elise. The other bowmen were below, trying to sleep, and a heavy silence hung in the night.

'Do you think your steward and the Norsemen will return before we are attacked, sire?' the bowman asked, in a voice scarcely more than a whisper.

'I wish I knew, Elise,' Madog answered. 'My mind would be the easier were I to know that this would be the case.'

The two spoke no more but remained standing motionless in the brooding night air. How long they stood there Madog did not know, and a dreamlike feeling crept over him. With a start, he felt Elise touch his arm and, narrowing his eyes against the gloom, he saw that the bowman was pointing across the marsh. At the far end of the causeway, a tiny spark of light was showing and, as he watched, it flared into a fire glow, to be followed by another and yet another, until the area around the old bathhouse glowed in the night sky. Cadwaladr's men had arrived and Madog wondered if today had been his last on this earth. He felt Elise stir beside him and, without thinking, he followed the other man's movement, crossing himself and commending his body into God's keeping.

5

The winter dawn found the causeway lying under a thick blanket of mist, which muffled sounds as well as hiding the opposite shore. Standing at the edge of dry land, Madog shivered in the chill air, and wished that he had brought a cloak, to combat the cold, as his eyes sought vainly to pierce the mist. In the company of his bowmen, he had spent a restless night, huddled close to a small fire in the tower, taking his turn outside, to listen for any warning sounds. Some movement from the tower caused him to glance behind him, and he saw his companions emerge through the low tower doorway.

'We are as blind men, Elise,' he remarked, when the bowman stood beside him. Muttering his thanks, he took a goblet offered to him by one of the others and sipped its contents. The mulled wine warmed him and he began to walk up and down the shore until he felt his limbs lose their stiffness. He then rejoined the others and for what seemed an age, the five men stared into the woolly whiteness, straining their ears for any sound. The noises which they eventually heard, though, came from the island road, not the causeway, and it was with relief that they saw Rhodri, followed by the now armed fishermen and farmers, emerge from the mist. Amongst them, Madog recognised the man he had left guarding Castell Morfa, and he nodded his approval when the man raised his long spear in salute.

'Apart from Owain, who still keeps watch out to sea, all your men are here, sire,' Rhodri told him. 'Has our foe arrived?'

'Indeed he has, though it was not until night had fallen,' Madog answered. 'By the count of their fires when they made camp, they must number many hundreds of men.'

He pointed to the piles of stones that had been wrenched from the causeway and now littered the ground.

'These stones should not be wasted, Rhodri. Have the men build a wall opposite the gap with them. They could offer some protection.'

His captain repeated the order to the waiting men, who stacked their weapons close to hand before beginning the task. They worked with a will and very soon had built a stout low wall from the stone. Passing the last one to the next man, Madog wondered who had handled the stone a millennium ago and what that person had looked like. With the wall completed, there was now a drop the height of a man to the surface of the marsh, and beneath that lay at least another two feet of gluey mud. Altogether, it made a formidable obstruction, though whether or not it would stop a determined horde of attackers remained to be seen. There was no more to be done now but await events. Madog stood aside as Rhodri sent the bowmen into the tower and formed the remaining men into line, then took his place in the centre.

Across the marsh, David, eldest son of Cadwaladr, completed the task of putting on his armour and then stepped through the open flap of his pavilion.

'It is not going to lift until warmed by the sun; we must needs wait until then,' another armoured figure told him, gesturing towards the mist.

David glanced at the white shroud hiding the marsh and then turned to his father's chief captain. Rhys ap Iorwerth cut an impressive figure in his black armour, which was designed to show off his bodily strength. His tone of voice warned against argument, and David kicked at the turf in anger.

'All the while, my brother draws nearer by sea,' he snarled. 'The taking of Moel-y-Gest must be mine and mine alone. I have had my fill of walking in another's shadow. We shall wait as you advise, for a while, then, mist or no mist, we shall attack before noon.'

Rhys glared at him for a few moments, then slowly shook his head.

'I will not lead men blindly into battle,' he said forcefully. 'Should you decide to proceed, you will do so without my help.'

David watched the captain walk stiffly away, half drew his sword then slammed it fiercely back into its scabbard. He had meant every word of his outburst, and was determined to back them up by action. Besides having to compete against Rhys in leadership, his younger brother, Griffith, had shown a natural talent for the art of war. Their father had often pointed out this fact, and it stung David deeply. The morning passed slowly and his nerves were almost at screaming point when the mist finally began to stir. He immediately gave the command for his men to form up, and then he went down to the causeway. By now, he could see some distance along the road, and he waited impatiently until his men-at-arms took their place in the van. Behind them and led by a standard-bearer, the remainder of his father's men made ready, and David took his place beside the flag. He saw that Rhys stood aside with the men of Powys. The captain made no move, and cursing under his breath, David gave the order to advance.

The men on Moel-y-Gest heard their approaching foe long before they sighted them. At this end of the causeway, the mist though now swirling in great clouds, still made it impossible to see further than fifty paces. The steady rhythm of booted feet, with an occasional clink of armour, grew louder at every passing moment, and Rhodri growled an order as, with mounting tension, men began to fidget. At the top of the tower, Elise notched an arrow and then held his breath as the first men-at-arms showed through the mist. The mailed soldiers were marching four abreast, shoulder to shoulder, their shields held at the ready.

'Hold fast, lads,' he said to his comrades. 'These men know what they are about. There will be easier targets following.'

His advice proved to be correct; as their enemy drew nearer, he saw a standard-bearer followed by a packed mass of spearmen appear through the whiteness. At his command, the bowmen drew back on their bowstrings and sent their arrows zipping through the air. At so short a range, they could not miss, and as the deadly darts struck home, the advancing ranks were thrown into confusion. As more arrows followed, in quick succession, many of the spearmen looked upward at the hissing noise, thus exposing their faces, their necks offering a soft target. Amongst the first to be hit was David, who, glancing up, was struck in the cheek. The impact knocked him backward and under the trampling feet of those following. In a short space, Elise and the other bowmen had shot sixty arrows into the milling front ranks, who began desperately to try to escape. Wildly pushing and punching at those behind them, their struggles added to the growing chaos, and as men began to fall into the marsh, panic took hold, and those at the rear began to flee.

Standing among his men, Madog felt a surge of elation as he watched his foe run back into the mist. The odds against him had changed dramatically and now only the men-at-arms faced his small force. With their shields held high, the leading rank of mailed men reached the gap in the road, paused briefly and then slithered down into the mire. The weight of their armour caused them to sink to their waists, yet gamely they struggled towards the bank. Their comrades followed, shouting encouragement to each other, and slowly they narrowed the gap between them and the wall.

'Make ready, lads,' Rhodri roared above the growing din. 'Show no mercy to any of them.'

Struggling against the clinging mud, the leading men-at-arms reached the bank, only to find themselves in a hopeless position. In vain, they tried to climb onto dry land, only to find that their heavy boots could not gain any purchase and that their swords could not reach their opponents. Madog's men, however, found it all too easy. Thrusting with their long spears, they knocked their closest foes off their feet, with terrible results. The weight of armour caused many of them to sink below the surface, and though a few managed to regain their feet, the majority did not reappear. The shouts of encouragement quickly turned to cries of warning, and while a few pressed on with the attack, the majority firstly wavered, then began to move back. So far, Madog had not raised a hand but now he leaned carefully over the wall. Directly below him, a man-at-arms was desperately trying to pull himself clear of the marsh. The man had discarded his shield and was using his heavy sword to lever himself upward, leaving himself fully exposed. With Rhodri's words fresh in his mind, Madog swung his sword high and then brought it crashing down on the helmeted head. The blow struck the man sideways and he fell heavily into the mire. Somehow, he kept his head above the surface and, frantically, he made for the relative safety of the causeway.

'You did well, lads,' Rhodri called out, as he watched the last of their foe join the retreating column. 'They will have to think up some other means of setting foot on this island. Rest for now and save your strength for what may come later.'

He motioned to Madog and led the young princeling aside.

'That affair could not have been easier, Sire,' he said in a low voice. 'We had but one man hurt, though I fear it will be a harder knock when they come again.'

'They have learned that they must show caution, though,' Madog replied. 'The longer they take, the more it suits us. If we can hold until night falls, the better is the chance that Eric will return.'

''Tis a gamble,' Rhodri replied, 'and yet, we really have no other choice than to do what is being done.'

Stifling a cry of pain, David squirmed from beneath the lifeless body of one of his men and glanced fearfully back at the tower. Through blood-clogged eyes, he could see that the ramparts were now empty of bowmen; thankfully, he lurched to his feet and began to run back along the causeway. His movements sent a searing pain through his head, yet not until he was hidden by the last wisps of mist did he come to a stop. When he had been struck down, he had pulled the arrow from his cheek, and now his left eye was swollen tightly. Gingerly, he touched the wound, and his hand came away sticky with blood. He felt himself sway with weakness and, making a huge effort, he forced himself to walk on towards safety. Before long, he could make out the mainland shore through the now rapidly evaporating mist, and saw a confused mass of men milling around by the water's edge. At the end of the causeway, a group of heavily armoured men were arguing amongst themselves and, as he drew closer, he saw, with a sinking feeling, that Rhys was among them.

'Well, now, young sir, it seems that you have learned a bitter lesson,' the captain cried out angrily. 'Your men came scampering back with fear in their eyes, not having struck a single blow. It was all we could do to stop their flight. Many of them are yet running around in circles.'

David lowered his head to hide his shame. He could not think of anything to say in reply, so, half blindly, he stumbled past the captain. He felt a restraining hand on his shoulder and squinted up into Rhys's face.

'You are fortunate to be alive, lad,' Rhys said in a milder tone. 'A little higher and that arrow would have pierced your eye and probably penetrated into your brain. Your attack, though foolish, has told us what to expect. I will order the men to fell trees that we can use to fill in that deadly gap at the other end'

He turned to his companions and called out, 'Two of you, help the lad to his pavilion and have a physician attend to his wound. The rest of you, get this rabble into some order.'

On the island, Madog's men were cheered by the arrival of some of their womenfolk. The wives and daughters carried baskets of food and drink, which they shared out amongst the grateful men. Chewing on a chicken leg, Madog realised, that he was famished; his only sustenance that day had been the goblet of mulled wine. 'My thanks to you, good women,' he shouted, between mouthfuls. 'There is one more task that you must do. Have everyone gather as much food together as they can carry and be ready to bring it down to the beach. I do not know when, but it could be any moment.'

At that moment, he would have given much for news of Eric. Later on, after some thought, he spoke with Rhodri.

'What if we sent a rider back to the beach, to watch for the Norsemen's return?' he asked. 'He could tell of our situation and then return here. The men would be encouraged to learn that the boats have arrived safely.'

The captain agreed and summoned a lad of some fourteen years to them.

'Your task is of great importance,' he told the boy, whose name was Tudor. 'The moment that you have informed their leader, Eric, that we have a fight on our hands and advised him to make ready to put to sea, ride swiftly back here. Your news could well save the day.'

The two men watched him ride away, mounted on Madog's pony, then they returned to the makeshift wall, both men deep in thought. Neither man knew that they were wondering about the same thing, which was whether, or not, they would yet be alive when the lad returned.

Shortly afterwards, they heard Elise call to them from the tower, and saw him gesturing to them to join him. Climbing the winding stairway, they joined the bowman, who pointed toward the far shore.

'There is much movement between their camp and that woodland to our right, Sire,' Elise told them. 'Our foes appear to be busy felling trees and dragging them back to their camp.'

'Probably collecting firewood,' Madog replied. 'They have to eat and it will take many camp fires to feed so many.'

'You may be right, Sire,' Elise said in a doubtful tone, 'and yet, the coming and going seems too orderly.'

The three watched the distant movements for a while until Rhodri suddenly swore and slapped the rampart with an open palm.

'That timber is not meant for any cooking use,' he snorted. 'I will wager that it is intended to fill the gap between our wall and the causeway.' He looked around the tower then spoke on. 'How many arrows have you left, Elise?' he asked.

'We have some three score, most of which we have recovered from the causeway,' the bowman answered. 'Once these have been loosed, we will have only our knives to fight with.'

'I fear that we shall be up against it, Sire,' Rhodri growled. 'Once the arrows have gone, our foes will be able to toss their logs into the marsh and bridge the gap. Who can tell for how long we can hold them with sword and pike? I'm not a deeply religious man, but I think now is a good moment to start praying.'

Close by the old Roman bathhouse, Rhys watched his men drag the fallen timber up to the causeway's entrance.

'Now, listen to me closely,' he ordered. 'I want every branch lopped off until only the smooth trunk remains. We cannot risk having men tripping over any obstacle. We have a hard enough task ahead of us as it is, so let us not add to our difficulties.'

He watched them wield their axes for a while, then he

walked a short distance along the causeway. Now that the mist had cleared, Moel-y-Gest stood out clearly, and he stared at the distant tower. From where he stood, the building looked tiny and insignificant, yet it posed a huge obstacle to his men.

Shrugging his powerful shoulders, he turned back toward the camp, feeling a warming breath on his face as he did so. The pale sun, which was already signalling the coming of dusk, held no heat, and as he looked around, he saw the marsh reeds gently ripple. He gave a grunt of pleasure as he walked on; a wind, even a breeze would keep that accursed mist away. He had been debating with himself as to when he would lead the next attack on the island, and now he made up his mind. It would be on the morrow, as soon as there was light enough.

6

Madog awoke from an exhausted sleep, his senses straining for signs of his foe. Getting to his feet, he looked over the marshland, toward their camp, becoming aware that there was no friendly mist and that the new day was noticeably warmer. At that moment, the causeway stood empty of life, and he prayed that it would stay that way a while longer. Several of his men were seated around a fire and one of them offered him a pot of warmed wine. Despite the growing tension in his stomach muscles, he sipped it down, welcoming the drink's warming glow.

''Tis going to be harder for us today, Sire,' the man said grimly. 'What are the chances of the Norsemen returning?'

'They will be here, Iorwerth,' Madog answered, trying to sound confident. 'We can count on them, of that I'm sure.' He drained the last of the sweetened wine and made his way through the other men, answering much the same question at each campfire. Entering the tower, he began to climb upward, disturbed by the thought that he would be responsible for the deaths of any of those below. When he came out onto the ramparts, he found that Rhodri was already there, talking to the bowmen. All of them were looking across the marsh and when he joined them, the captain glanced at him.

'They are making ready, Sire,' he said. 'There is much movement in their camp, though, at this distance, 'tis not clear what they are about.'

Across the marsh, Rhys was drawing his men into order. At first, all was confusion, until they saw clearly what he wanted of them. With a file of men-at-arms at either side, two files of men took their places in the centre, carrying logs. Behind these he placed some fifty bowmen, with his pike men bringing up the rear. When all were drawn up to his satisfaction, he began to take off the few pieces of armour that he was wearing.

'You men-at-arms, shed your chain-mail coats,' he called out. 'We lost good men yesterday through carrying too much weight. Your swords and shields will suffice for this day's business.'

A slight commotion came from the bowmen as they parted to allow someone to pass through and, with a twinge of annoyance, the captain saw David approach.

'I am coming with you, Rhys,' the young man told him. 'I command this army and shall have the honour of leading it to victory.'

The captain fought back the urge to tell David to clear off, knowing that a snub now would never be forgotten or forgiven. Forcing a smile, he looked into the other's still swollen face.

'Very true, my lord,' he replied. 'I would welcome your help. May I suggest that you place yourself at the head of the main body? From there, you can strike the decisive blow. I shall assist the logging party.'

He waited until David's banner fluttered in front of the pike men, then drew his sword and ordered the advance.

'They are coming, Sire,' Rhodri said in a grim voice. 'We had best move down and prepare.'

Madog nodded but did not follow his captain immediately. Instead, he moved closer to the bowmen.

'Much depends on your skill,' he told them. 'Shoot your arrows straight, make every one of them count. When all have been used, join us below.'

They nodded and began to notch their bowstrings.

'May God be with you,' he added, as he headed for the steps.

Rhodri had already drawn the men up behind the wall and

he joined them, taking his place in the line, several paces from the captain. The men on either side of him glanced his way and he smiled at them, hoping that the apprehension he felt did not show in his face.

At a steady pace, Rhys walked along the causeway, the sound of marching feet growing louder as more and more men reached the stone road. Slowly but surely the distance between the opposing sides narrowed, and as he drew closer, Rhys kept his eyes riveted on the tower. With less than a hundred paces to go, there was a sudden movement from the ramparts, and he saw the flash of arrows shoot towards his men. Yelling a warning, he raised his shield high, to protect both himself and the man next to him, but he heard them pass by overhead. They fell amongst his bowmen and, shouting at the top of his lungs, he ordered them to shoot back.

Elise watched his comrades' arrows strike home, and paused to see what their foes would do in answer. His curiosity almost cost him his life as an arrow zipped past his ear, followed by a shower of the missiles, which clattered about the tower like hail. 'God's Blood! Those men of Powys know their archery,' he thought. Below him, Madog and his men crouched behind the wall and, with immense relief, he saw four more arrows streak from the ramparts. For some moments, the air was filled with the deadly darts, and the screams of stricken men were added to the growing din. Turning to his front, Madog saw that their foes had now reached the gap, and from under the protecting shields, two logs were pitched into the marsh.

On Rhys's command, more logs were passed along to the men at the front, and these were quickly added to the first, until the timber could be seen just below the surface. Pleased that his plan was working, Rhys shouted encouragement to his men, urging them to work faster, then, holding his breath, he stepped off the causeway, Although the logs were slippery, he managed to keep to his feet moving slowly forward as log after log went into the water.

The men of Moel-y-Gest watched helplessly as their enemies drew closer, waiting nervously for them to come within reach of their pikes. It was as one of them tentatively lunged at Rhys that the thud of hooves came to their ears.

'The ships are here; they are here,' Tudor's voice, high pitched with excitement, rang out.

The lad reined his blowing pony to a skidding halt and ran to Madog's side.

'The Norsemen came in with the beginning of the new tide, Sire,' he yelled above the noise. 'They towed the other ship up-river as far as they could before anchoring.

Madog's spirits soared with joy at Tudor's news, and his men cheered wildly as the news spread amongst them. Should they be unable to repulse their foes, they might yet be able to make a fighting retreat to the beach. It was only a faint chance that they would succeed, yet at least it gave them some hope.

While his men had secured the long-ship, with difficulty, Eric had made sense of what Tudor had told him. The lad was so excited that his words tumbled out faster than the Norseman could follow them. It was plain that something had happened during his absence, and this was confirmed when he saw the island's women and children hurrying down to the beach. The lad's pony skittered as a wavelet splashed its hooves, and he grabbed its mane, to hold the animal steady.

'Your master is in trouble?' he asked.

Tudor nodded. 'Cadwaladr's men are here,' he answered, slowing his speech. 'There was a short fight yesterday, which we won. Madog asks that you help the women to get aboard and make ready to sail. I must go and tell him of your arrival.'

Eric watched the lad ride away and then he clambered back

onto the long ship, using its planked walkway to make his way to the stern. At both ends of the craft there were covered storerooms; opening the rear one, Eric rummaged through its contents. When, finally, he turned around, he was holding a round shield, a battle-axe and a helmet in his hands. Immediately, he saw that his men were watching him intently.

'My friend has a fight on his hands,' he told them. 'I think that he may need my help. 'Tis no concern of yours, yet you are welcome to join me. It's been a while since we joined in battle and I wonder if we Norsemen are still as eager for combat as we once were.'

'Move away from the locker, Eric,' a man named Wolfstan called out in answer. 'Your friends are ours. That apart, you may be good in a scrap but you will still need us to watch out for you.'

There was a rush to get to the locker as Eric, grinning widely, leapt ashore and ran to where the other ship had anchored, opposite the beached fishing boats. From the direction of the headland, he saw another horseman galloping towards him and he waited until the rider drew rein beside him. Ignoring the man for the moment, Eric called out to those on the ship.

'Torberg, listen to me. We are away to help the young Welshman. You and the others, get these people on board. Use these fishing boats to carry them across.' Turning now to Owain, he spoke in broken Welsh.

'Take a boat over to my men and help them in their work. There are four of them aboard with your master's servant, Cynon.'

Owain's first reaction was to refuse. His lifelong friend was in great danger and he was desperate to go to his aid. The sea remained empty of ships along the peninsula and he had not been able to contain his anxiety any longer. Eric saw the young man's brow crease in a frown, and spoke on.

'You will do Madog a greater service by helping here,' he said. 'He will be the stronger for knowing that his people are safe.'

Owain saw the sense in the Norseman's words and nodded in agreement. The two men pushed a fishing boat into the water and he leapt aboard. Owain began to row, managing a hasty wave at Helen, who stood amongst the other women on the beach.

At the causeway, Rhys's men had now reached the wall. The thrusting pikes had felled several of his men-at-arms but, following his example, the others pressed forward. Deflecting a pike with his shield, the captain closed in, swinging his sword at his opponent's body. The man leapt back nimbly, but before Rhys could haul himself over the wall, the space was filled by Rhodri. With a resounding clash, their swords and shields met. They clashed repeatedly as each man parried and thrust. The din grew even louder as, along the line, more men joined in combat. Free of their weighty chain mail, the men-at-arms spread along the water's edge until they over-lapped the wall, but for all their determination, the defenders held them back. Breathing in short gasps and his arms already feeling the weight of his sword, Madog hacked away at his foe below. From the corner of his eye, he saw one, and then two of his men stagger from the line and fall heavily to the ground. He wondered how much longer they could hold. Now was not the moment to turn and run for the beach. Their opponents would be on his men like a pack of wolves. He had a glimpse of Elise and the bowmen joining the fight, before he had to parry another slashing sword.

It was at this moment that David ordered his men forward. By sheer weight of numbers, they pushed the surviving bowmen aside and began to slither over the logs. For a moment, his swollen eyes searched along the line of defenders, until they came to rest on Madog, conspicuous in his mail coat. Ignoring everything else, he stepped into the marsh and began to wade towards his target. Following Rhys's command, he had freed himself of his heavy armour and found that he was able to move steadily through the mire. In a few moments, he had reached the bank, and looked up into the face of his intended victim. Madog was battling with a man-at-arms and, as he parried a blow with his shield, David saw his chance. With all the strength in his legs, he flung himself forward, his arms held wide. His attention fully focussed on his opponent, Madog knew nothing of the danger until he felt David's arms wrap around his legs. He felt something give him a quick jerk and, before he could do anything to save himself, he slid helplessly into the marsh, losing his sword as he did so. For a frightening moment, he looked up into David's triumphant face, aware of the sword poised high in readiness to strike, then, he almost screamed, as his foe's head seemed to burst in a welter of blood.

A strong hand grasped his coat, pulled him clear of the marsh and dumped him on the bank. He had to choke back another scream when he saw the cause of his rescue, for, towering above him stood Eric, bloodied axe in his hand, and on his head a frightening helmet. It had wings on either side, and metal bars protected his cheeks and nose. The big man looked like an apparition from Hell. Madog became aware of a rush of men sweeping past, and saw a tightly bunched group of Norsemen jump into the marsh and smash into the enemy.

The screams of dying and wounded men rang high above the din, so loudly that Rhys risked a glance to see the cause. It was the last move he ever made for, as quick as lightening, Rhodri brought his sword swinging down on the other man's exposed neck. The deaths of both their commanders and the fear of the Norsemen's awesome axes stopped Cadwaladr's army in its tracks. Those at the rear began to move back, leaving those at the front isolated.

Bellowing an order to charge, Rhodri led his men over the wall and splashed madly up to their dwindling foes. A few moments later, the battle was over, when islanders and Norse met, and their enemies were retreating along the causeway.

'My thanks to you, Eric,' Madog gasped. 'I owe you my life and the lives of my men. How can I ever repay you?'

'Your friendship is payment enough,' Eric answered with a smile. 'Though, let's not linger here in talk, young sir. We had best make for the ships, now that we have the chance.'

He turned away, called to his men to re-group and then glanced back, 'Who knows what awaits us in the days ahead? You may yet risk your neck for me.'

Madog heard Rhodri order their men together and, getting to his feet, he forced his trembling legs to walk over to the captain. The soldier took off his helmet and wiped the sweat from his brow, aware that his hand was shaking noticeably. He had experienced a number of sword fights over the years, though none had been as furious as this last one. His opponent had been a worthy adversary, and Rhodri knew that he was fortunate to be unscathed. He saw Madog look about him at the bodies of friend and foe, which lay all around.

'We were fortunate again today, Sire,' he said.' We lost but three men, though there are but a few of us who escaped injury.'

At Eric's insistence, Madog led his men away first, with the Norsemen bringing up the rear. Looking over his shoulder, he saw them stumble wearily along the track, and he knew that they were in no state to fight again that day. One of them sank to his knees. Madog dismounted and helped the man to climb onto the pony's back.

'Get me to the beach, Sire,' the farmer said weakly. 'My family await us and they will care for me.'

Slowly and painfully, the column moved along until, finally, they came out of the trees and onto the sands. At the water's edge, Owain and the four Norsemen were waiting anxiously, each man standing by a fishing boat. Aboard the ship, Madog could see the strained faces of the womenfolk, as their eyes searched amongst his men, and he dreaded the moment when the dead were missed. Again, Eric took command.

'Get your badly wounded onto the ship,' he told Madog gently.' Go with them, as they will need someone to give them orders. Your soldiers must come with me, for I need their strength, tired though they may be. The tide is not yet full and the breeze is against us, so we shall have to tow you out to sea.'

At first glance, the ship was smaller than Madog had hoped for, though its lines were much the same as the long-ship's. Clambering over its side from one of the boats, he saw that it had a much wider beam and, being partly decked, offered a surprising amount of space.

'You have bought wisely, Cynon,' he said, greeting his old steward with a smile. 'The ship is roomier than it appears.'

'I thought it suitable, Sire,' Cynon replied. 'The cost was fair and I wasted not a moment in seeking any other. We still have monies left, which we shall surely need.' He examined Madog from head to toe and then asked, 'You are not hurt in any way, Sire?'

'Only my pride,' Madog answered. 'Though, were it not for Eric, I would not be here now.'

With the help of the four Norsemen, the ship was soon ready to sail, and Eric drew the long-ship alongside. A stout rope was passed over and secured at the bow, and, with straining arms, the oarsmen got under way. Trying hard not to listen to the cries of those who had lost their loved ones, Madog watched the fishing boats fall into line. He leaned on the stern-rail and watched the beach slide by, the abandoned ponies the only living creatures on the deserted sands. As the distance from the land slowly grew, he saw Castell Morfa through the bare trees, and a painful surge of sadness ran through him. The thought that he would never see his home again filled his eyes with tears and, with a low groan, he forced himself to turn away. The strength of the tide slackened as the estuary filled, and the speed of the tiny armada increased, propelled by tiring arms. At long last, they came out onto the open sea and, pulling clear of the hidden sandbank, Eric turned southward. They had not been long on this course when a cry rang out. Looking toward the bow, Madog saw Tudor pointing to the north-west. Looking in this direction, he made out the sails of three ships in the far distance. Griffith, the surviving son of Cadwaladr, had finally made an appearance. He was about to call a warning to Eric when he saw the great sail hoisted high. From the centre of the long-ship, a boom was swung outward, moving the sail until it began to fill with the starboard breeze. Eric himself took over the heavy steering paddle, and using his strength, he brought the long-ship back on course. Madog felt his ship pick up speed immediately. Before long, the enemy sails were out of sight, and he heaved a deep sigh of relief. He and his people were safe, although heading into the unknown.

7

Brittany

The long-ship's bow ground over the fine sand and came to rest a few paces from the narrow stretch of beach. Within moments, its crew, Norse and Welsh, had waded ashore and secured the craft. A short distance behind, the *Moel-y-Gest* dropped its heavy anchor, its passengers gazing eagerly landward. It was they who had insisted on the name for the new ship, and Madog had been only too happy to agree. One by one, the little fishing boats entered the snug cove, drew alongside and began to ferry its passengers across to the beach. Amongst the first to land, Madog walked over to Eric and Rhodri, feeling the land dip and rise as he did so. They had spent three days and two nights at sea since leaving Cornwall, and his senses were in rhythm with his ship's motion. He glanced across the beach at the dense woodland, and wondered what reception they would receive from the local inhabitants. More welcoming than Pembroke and Cornwall, he hoped. Although the people in this part of southern Wales had allowed them ashore, they had made it plain that the northerners could not stay. Pembroke was within reach of Cadwaladr, and they wanted no trouble with the new Prince. Once the wounded had been properly attended to, the travellers had sailed on. When they reached the shores of Cornwall, they had met with more hostility. Scarcely had the first Norseman stepped ashore when a large body of mounted soldiers had appeared on the nearby cliff top. Their intention was made clear when, reaching the beach, the riders levelled their lances and prepared to charge. In haste, Madog and Eric had turned their ships about and, followed by the fishing boats, had sought the safety of the sea. It. was Rhodri who gave the reason for such a warlike act.

'They are Normans, Sire,' he had called out. 'I had no idea that they had come this far west.'

At the moment, there was no sign of life around the cove, and Madog expressed his hopes to the two men when he joined them.

'The women and children are greatly in need of hot food and rest,' he said. 'I pray that when our arrival has been discovered, we shall be made welcome.'

'We will not have to wait long to find out,' Eric said, looking over Madog's shoulder. 'Our presence has just been noted.'

Madog looked in the direction at which that the big man was now pointing, and saw a horse and rider, motionless at the edge of the trees. The horseman was watching them intently and, when the three men started to walk towards him, he wheeled the horse around and quickly disappeared from sight.

'What now, Sire?' Rhodri asked. 'It may be wise to prepare for trouble. We have no chance to defend ourselves, with everyone spread out over the beach.'

Madog thought for a few moments and then shook his head.

'We will not show any sign of hostility,' he replied. 'However, call the people together, then we must wait and see what happens.'

When everyone had drawn together, a silence fell over the crowd and all eyes focussed anxiously on the trees. Their wait was a short one for, after some movement in the wood, five .horsemen rode clear before coming to a halt. For a long while, no-one moved, while both groups studied each other until, finally, Madog tugged Eric's sleeve and began to walk across the sand. When they were a few paces from the horsemen, he

halted and was about to speak, when one of the riders called out.'
'Welcome to Armorica. May I ask the purpose of your visit?'

Madog looked up at the handsome figure in amazement. The man's speech, though he spoke in a strange accent, was perfectly clear to him.

'We are in need of food and rest,' he answered, speaking slowly. 'We intend no harm to any man. We have travelled far in search of a new homeland and our women and children are weary.'

The spokesman's face showed his surprise and then lightened in a broad smile. 'This is truly wondrous. Your speech is somewhat strange to my ear, though I understand much of what you say,' he said. He looked at the people on the beach for a few moments and then asked, 'Are you from the island of Britain?'

'Indeed, we are,' Madog answered. 'Our homeland is called Cymru; it lies in the west of the island.'

'Then, we are of the same people,' the other exclaimed. 'Our folklore tells us of this, though it is sad that this relationship has dwindled over the years.' He stared at Eric and then looked at the Norsemen on the beach. 'There is no need to ask who your companion is,' he said. 'How is it that you travel in such unlikely company?'

Madog briefly explained the events at Moel-y-Gest, then added, 'We owe our lives to the Norseman. He has helped us more than words can express.'

'Then, they and your people are equally welcome,' the horseman said warmly. He turned to the young man at his side and spoke on. 'Alain, will you and the others escort these travellers to our lodge. I shall go on ahead with these two and warn the servants to prepare for their arrival, and be sure to collect our kill. There must be more than one hundred souls on that beach in need of food. We shall need every scrap to fill their bellies.'

He waited until his companions rode onto the beach, then gestured to Madog and Eric to follow him. A little used track wound its way through the trees and, as he guided his mount along, he called back, 'We have been hunting earlier and have been rewarded with three good-sized boars. By the coming of night, your people will be dining on roasted meat,'

They followed the twisting track for some distance, until finally, it led onto an open area of pasture. In the centre, stood a large, sturdy building. In the far distance, Madog could make out a cluster of rooftops. As they neared the building, a number of people, who he guessed were servants, appeared and awaited their arrival. That the horseman was a person of significance was made clear by the respect that the servants showed him. Within moments of their arrival, the three men were seated on a bench, sipping from goblets containing rich, red wine.

'I should have made myself known to you,' said their host to Madog. 'My name is Roland and, for my sins, I am Lord of these lands. This place is one of my hunting lodges, but my duties brought me here this day. I have to give judgement on a bunch of rascals who have made life a misery for those living in these parts.'

He broke off in order to send one of the servants to the village.

'Tell them to bring me bread and wine,' he told the man. 'Inform them that I have one hundred guests to feed, Paul. Be polite but firm in your manner.'

He watched the man depart before he turned once more to Madog.

'You made a bold decision, when you fled your homeland with all your people,' he said. 'They must hold you in great esteem, to follow you in such a venture. I wonder if mine would do as much for me.'

He fell silent, turning the thought over in his mind, until the first of Madog's people came into view. In a moment, he was on his feet, giving orders to the servants, some of whom began to prepare cooking fires. Shortly after all had arrived, a number of villagers appeared, bringing bread, wine and vegetables. The scene about the hunting lodge was soon transformed into one of great activity, as the food was prepared. While this was going on, Madog mingled with his people, talking with them and giving encouragement where needed. He also spoke with the wounded, most of whom were on the mend, though one of the pike men was still in pain from a sword cut.

'I fear that I must seek another occupation, Sire,' he remarked ruefully.' My marching days are over. The trouble is, soldiering is the only trade I know.'

Madog was at a loss for words of advice, and mumbled encouragement as he moved on.

When night fell, the scene changed once more. The women and children had departed with the villagers, who willingly accepted Roland's command to provide them with shelter for the night. The only signs that a feast had taken place were the glowing embers of the fires around which the men now lay or sat. Seated between Elise and his captain, Madog stared into the glow with heavy eyes. Beside him, Rhodri, who had wined and dined with the best of the Norsemen, gave a satisfied belch before turning to Madog.

'So far, so good,' he said. 'What happens now?'

Madog tried hard to think of an answer but his tired mind refused to function. He sat in silence for a while, and was spared any further effort, when Rhodri's gentle snores reached his ears. He pulled his cloak tightly around him, lay down on the grass and, closing his eyes, drifted into sleep. His last thought was of Eric and his intended search for a new world.

The following morning, Roland summoned Madog to his lodge. On his arrival, the young Welshman found the nobleman holding the reins of two horses.

'I have given your situation some thought,' Roland said. 'I want you to accompany me, as I wish to show you something that could be of help.'

Mounting up, he led off in the opposite direction to the village. The two rode side by side, relaxing in the fine morning sunshine. The countryside reminded Madog of Wales, for it also had clear, running streams, woodlands and pastures, and only the mountains were missing.

'It is truly a wonder that we can understand one another,' Roland remarked, after a while. 'There can be no doubt that we are of the same people. We call our land Armorica, though our neighbours, the French, have named it Brittany. It could well be that they are more correct than we in their choice of name.'

They rode on in contented silence until the familiar smell of the sea came to them, and Roland spurred his horse into a gallop. Before long, they came to a sand and shingle beach, and here Roland drew rein and dismounted. He waited until Madog joined him and then led the way down to the water's edge, where he turned to face inland.

'This is what I wanted you to see,' he said.' Let us take a walk and look more closely at the land. I would like you to tell me what you think of it.'

Together, they made their way along the beach and Madog studied the scene. Almost at the centre of the bay, a stream carved its way through the shingle and down to the sea. At each end of the beach, rugged cliffs thrust seaward, giving protection to the bay itself. Several up-turned fishing boats lay above the high-water-mark and Roland told him that they belonged to some of the villagers. The overall picture was one of tranquillity, and it was only when they moved inland that this impression was marred. A short distance from the beach, the blackened ruins of what had once been a village cast an ugly scar on the land.

'Your Norseman's ancestors did this,' Roland said, before Madog could ask the question. 'Twice our people rebuilt their homes, and twice more they were looted and burned. In the end, they decided to move inland and out of sight from the sea.'

He seated himself on what had been a corner stone of a dwelling, and looked directly into Madog's eyes.

'Your people are welcome to settle here if they so wish,' he said. 'It's good land going to waste. My only demand is that they give me one tenth of their harvest, as my own people do.' He stretched his arms and shoulders to ease his muscles, then he added, 'On the morrow, I must attend to those rascals. The following day, I shall have to return to my castle. Let me know your decision by then.'

Taken aback by such a generous offer, Madog began to stammer out his heartfelt thanks but Roland waved his words aside.

'The Norsemen and your soldiers are another matter,' he said. 'Should word get around that I have such men at my call, my neighbours could cause me much trouble. They must leave my lands and the sooner the better, for all.'

His manner, though polite, was quite firm, and Madog sensed that it would be folly to discuss the matter any further. As the two were riding back to the hunting lodge, he told the nobleman of Eric's intention to seek a new world across the seas. His brow raised in disbelief, Roland stared at the young man.

'Those Norsemen are truly mad,' he said. 'We all know that the edge of our world lies somewhere out there. He and his men will be sailing to their deaths. I trust that you have no such wild ideas.'

'During these past weeks, I have thought no further than what the morrow would bring,' Madog replied, 'although, I have much to think about now.'

Later that day, he called the people together and told them of Roland's offer. Their faces showed their relief at the prospect. Their attitude, however, became one of concern, when they learned that the soldiers would have to leave. Secretly praying that no-one would ask his own intentions, Madog told them that, on the morrow, they would go and inspect their possible new land.

'It is good land and I have money enough to buy you seeds and tools for planting,' he told them. 'I am sure that you will find happiness here.'

He called Cynon and Rhodri to his side and began to walk toward the path that ran through the woods. He knew that Eric was already at the cove; his friend was never happy when away from his long-ship. They found and followed the twisting track for a while, and it was then that Rhodri asked the pressing question.

'Should the people decide to stay here, what is to happen to my men and myself? We are not men of the sea and have no knowledge of how to handle a ship. Where are we to go?'

'That, my friend, is what we are about to find out,' Madog answered. 'I owe Eric a great deal, not to mention my life. It would seem that now is the moment to repay some of that debt.'

The further he walked, the more certain he became of the idea that had come to him when he and Roland had spoken together. The thought of abandoning Eric and Rhodri was one that he could not entertain. Yet the decision would have to be made by the Norseman. When, finally, the three came to the cove, Madog called out a greeting to Eric, who was working on the long-ship with some of his men. The blonde giant waved back, leapt ashore and met them on the beach.

'We are ensuring that our repairs are holding together,' he

told them. 'I'm pleased to say that all seems to be well.'

He found a comfortable place and sat down with his back against a rock, then looked questioningly at Madog.

'What brings you here?' he asked. 'I thought that you would have much to attend to with your people.'

Madog seated himself and told the Norseman of Roland's offer of land.

'I think that we could search for an age and not find better,' he said. 'Rhodri and his men must move on, however. Their presence here could cause suspicion amongst Roland's neighbours. The same applies to you, my friend.'

Eric smiled and shrugged his massive shoulders.

'I can understand his reasoning,' he said, 'not that it matters. Should you and your people decide to stay, then it will be back up north to Ireland for me, to find more men. There are only thirty-eight of us now, which is not enough to handle that beauty with safety.' He gestured to the long-ship and added, 'It takes at least fifty oarsmen to ensure that.'

Madog looked across at the two ships for a while, then turned to Eric and asked, 'What if Rhodri, myself and his men came with you?'

A stunned silence, broken only by a loud gasp from Rhodri, fell over the others. For several moments, no-one spoke, until finally, Eric's mouth widened in a grin.

'I'm beginning to think that it was fate as well as the storm that brought me to your shores,' he said. 'My destiny and yours seem to be drawing us closer with every passing day. I tell you, my friend, nothing would please me more than to have you with us on our journey.' Madog turned then to Rhodri, whose face still showed his surprise.

'There you have it, my captain,' he said.' I shall be going with Eric, come what may. Keeping in mind that I shall no longer be your employer, are you willing to follow me?'

'I beg you to give me a while to think the matter over, Sire,' Rhodri answered. 'At the moment, my mind is in turmoil, and I must also speak with the men about it. I cannot command them to join you in such an adventure. Each man will have to make his own decision. I shall talk with them when we return to the lodge.'

He frowned in thought for a while longer, and Madog saw the captain's eyes begin to gleam with excitement.

'Truly what you ask of me does have much appeal. It would be a wondrous adventure, seeking for a new world.' He picked up a dead twig and snapped it with his fingers, then added, 'that is, if one really does exist.'

'Oh, but it does, Rhodri, Eric said convincingly. 'Our people know of lands which lie in the far north, across a great sea. There is no reason why there should not be land further south.'

The three Welshmen agreed to meet with Eric later, at the hunting lodge, and set off back along the twisting path. They had not gone far when Cynon caught hold of Madog's sleeve and pulled him to a halt.

'What of me, Sire? Where is my place in your plans?' he asked. Madog looked fondly at his steward and saw the old man's earnest look.

'Your place would be here,' he answered. 'The people will be in need of a wise head to advise them on matters. Who better than you, old friend.'

'Never,' Cynon's voice rang out.' I have served your family for most of my life and nothing will ever prevent me from carrying on that duty. I am going with you, no matter where.'

Taken aback by Cynon's resolute manner, Madog searched for the right words to say that might change his steward's mind. The need quickly vanished, however, as, brushing past him, the old man took the lead.

'Come along, Madog. We have much to attend to.'

Without another word, Madog obeyed, with a smile on his lips. The incident reminded him of occasions back at Castell Morfa, when, after some youthful prank, the steward had chastised him. For a few moments, he felt as though he were a carefree lad once more.

Later, with the coming of dusk, the men, Welsh and Norse, gathered around a huge fire. The married men had departed to the village with their families. Cynon had shared a handful of silver coins amongst them.

'These are to pay your hosts,' he had told them. 'We must not be a burden on their backs.'

Before he sat down, Madog glanced around the gathering, seeking for Rhodri. His captain was talking earnestly with his men, and Madog could clearly see the surprise showing on some of their faces. Seated next to Eric, he waited in silence for a while, until he felt the Norseman begin to fidget in impatience. Finally, the Norseman called out,' Have your men come to a decision, Rhodri? I must know their intentions tonight. My own plans cannot wait any longer.'

Aware that all eyes were on him, the captain got to his feet and squinted through the fire's glow.

'There is no place for me back in Wales,' he said.' I would surely fall foul of Cadwaladr one day. I am willing to join you. As for these poor souls, they all agree that they would be lost without my guiding hand. Apart from Iwan, they will join you to a man. He doubts that his wound will ever heal and says that he needs the care of a good woman.'

His soldiers hooted with laughter at his remark, some shouting lewd comments at the unfortunate man, who grinned sheepishly back at them. Madog was both relieved and pleased at what he had heard; relieved that the men had agreed to accompany him and pleased with their high morale.

'It seems that you have your crew, Eric,' he said. 'They know little of the sea but are all stout fellows.'

His friend gave a nod. 'True enough. They will learn quickly; of that I am sure,' he said. 'Now, I have another question. What do you plan to do with the *Moel-y-Gest*? It could well be wise if she sailed with us. She can hold much in the way of food and water, when we set off across the great sea.'

Madog mentally kicked himself, for in truth, he had not given a single thought to his own ship.

'What you say makes good sense,' he replied.' We shall use her as you suggest.' 'Then, we are agreed,' Eric confirmed,' and although it will be difficult to crew the two ships, it will not be impossible.'

When Madog settled down to sleep that night, it was with a feeling of mounting excitement. The thoughts of sailing the seas and finding a strange but wonderful new land filled his mind. Only one question now remained. Would the people of Moel-y-Gest decide to settle here in Brittany?

By noon the following day, he had his answer. Earlier, he had led them to the ruined village and pointed out the land that Roland had offered. Their immediate response was promising and then, as they looked more closely at the land, their enthusiasm grew even more.

'The soil is truly rich, Sire,' one of them told him. 'It is better than back home, and would you look at the grass. A man could feed cattle on it even though spring has not yet arrived.'

Later, Madog called them all together and spoke to them as friends and no longer tenants.

'I believe that God himself led us here,' he said. 'There is fresh water, timber and land in plenty. My hope is that you will accept Roland as your new lord. I have no doubts that you will prosper and be happy here.'

There was a loud cry of agreement to what he had said, although one of the farmers raised a hand and called for silence.

'What about you, Madog?' the man asked. 'Rumour has it that you are going to sail with the Norsemen.'

'The rumour is true enough, my friend,' Madog answered. 'I believe that I have fulfilled my obligation to you. I must now do likewise towards Rhodri and Eric. If it were not for them, none of us would be here today.'

'We have spoken together about the matter,' the spokesman replied. 'We wish you a safe voyage to wherever you are bound, and pray that someday you will return to us.'

The people began to move away, each family anxious to choose their own land, leaving Madog with three young fishermen.

'We wish to speak with you,' one of them said. 'We have discussed matters between us and wish to sail with you, that is, if you are willing to take us.'

Madog looked at them in some surprise and then smiled broadly.

'Indeed, I will,' he said warmly. 'Your knowledge of sailing will be most welcome. I must warn you, however, that we shall be going into the unknown, and could be faced with many dangers.'

The three grinned back at him.

'No more dangerous than the fight at the causeway,' one of them replied. 'We survived that and hold no fear of what lies out there.' He pointed a hand out to sea and, as he did so, the long-ship and the *Moel-y-Gest* appeared around the headland.

Amongst the first to land, Eric hurried over to Madog and asked anxiously, 'Have your people reached a decision? I have scarcely thought of anything else all morning.' Madog told him of the outcome of the meeting and of the offer of the three fishermen.

'There is nothing to hold us now,' he said. 'We can leave whenever you are ready.'

Eric led him away from the approaching Norsemen and spoke of something that had nagged at him all that morning.

'We can buy all the food these Bretons can spare us,' he said. 'There is no problem on that account. What concerns me is that, even with your three fishermen, we shall be short of men. It will take at least ten to sail your ship, and I shall be short of oarsmen when we head into the open sea. Maybe we can pick up more men on our way further south. It is a chance we shall have to take.'

On the way back to the hunting lodge, Madog turned the problem over in his mind. It was as he drew near that a thought struck him. He saw Elise and his bowmen busily fashioning arrows and he asked them if Roland had returned from conducting the trial. They answered that the nobleman was still at the village. At this, Madog hurried over to the spare horses, which were tethered to a picket line. Not bothering to saddle up, he untied one of the animals, grabbed its mane, and hauled himself onto its back. By using the strength of one arm, he turned his mount's head and set off at a run for the village.

As he drew near, he saw a large crowd gathered in an open space. He dismounted and pushed his way through the press. Ignoring their cries of protest, he broke clear, coming to a stop when he saw what lay before him. A large tree stood in the centre of the clearing; from its lower branches six noosed ropes hung. Nearby, a number of armed men stood guarding a small group of manacled figures, and Madog ran over to them. At his demand as to Roland's whereabouts, one of the guards pointed to a nearby building. Aware of the need for haste, Madog hurried over, brushed past a sentry, opened a door and entered.

His unannounced arrival caused those inside to swivel in their chairs and stare at him.

Roland had been speaking and, after breaking off for a moment, he continued, 'I understand your wish to be rid of these men, yet their misdoings are not that evil. They have not even threatened to harm any man. They are no more than petty thieves. I agree that this thievery must stop. How we do this I do not know; maybe hanging is the only answer, though I am loathe to carry out such a sentence.'

His audience looked, at each other in some dismay and, seizing the moment, Madog spoke out.

'My lord, may I be allowed to speak?' he asked. At Roland's nod, he went on. 'I believe that I can offer a solution to your problem. My people have agreed to accept your generous offer of land, which means that my soldiers and the Norsemen can now leave. However, we need more men to handle the vessels. Were you to release these six rogues into my custody, they will be gone from Brittany on the morrow.'

Some of the villagers muttered in dissent when Madog's suggestion was made clear to them, though the young Welshman could see that Roland liked the idea. The nobleman would welcome the early departure of the foreign fighting men.

'What you say makes sense,' Roland said in reply. He got to his feet and placed a hand on the hilt of his sword. 'The miscreants will serve a purpose,' he told the others. 'My judgement is that they are to be handed over to Madog. From what he has told me, there is little or no chance that we shall ever see them again.'

Several of those present began to mutter amongst themselves, and at this, Roland's voice took on a steel-like tone.

'This is my command. Let no man here disobey me.'

The grumbling voices immediately stopped and, motioning Madog to follow him, Roland strode out of the room.

'You would make a clever ambassador to any court,' he told

Madog, when they were outside. 'You have both pleased me and got what you wanted.'

He ordered Alain to escort the prisoners to the hunting lodge, and, as Madog mounted his horse, he smiled up at the young man.

'We shall both be busy on the morrow and may not see each other again,' he said. 'I think that you are mad to embark on this venture of yours, though I wish you well. Rest assured, your people will be treated as fairly as my own. May God go with you, Madog.'

As Madog rode back, he overtook a lad of some twelve years, who raised a tearful face as he rode by. The picture of despair caused him to draw rein and, leaning down, he spoke to the boy.

'What is the cause of your misery?' he asked kindly.

'I am losing my father,' the boy sobbed. 'He is one of the prisoners. I have no mother and will be alone in the world.'

The lad's grief touched Madog's heart and, acting on impulse, he held out a hand.

'Then, I must stop the cause of your sorrow,' he said. 'Give me your hand and I promise that you will be with your father.'

With a heave, he swung the boy up behind him and, with his passenger holding tight, he rode on. Madog realised after a while why he had acted as he had done. The lad's plight reminded him so much of his own feelings on the day that his parents had died.

Well before noon on the following day, Madog stood at the stern of the *Moel-y-Gest*. On the beach, the people stood gathered to watch his departure. He searched his mind yet again, although he knew by now that he had done all that he could do for them. He had learned that Owain had decided to stay in Brittany with his sweetheart, Helen. The news came as no surprise to him, though he did have feelings of regret at the loss of a lifelong friend. Without hesitation, he had appointed Owain spokesman for the people and handed the new leader a purse full of coins.

'That is to enable you to buy food and seed,' he had told Owain. 'There is more than enough for that purpose.'

He gave a last look around the ship and then ordered the heavy anchor to be raised. The crew, made up of Welsh and Norsemen, heaved the iron hook on board, and slowly the ship moved away from land on the ebb tide. Madog saw the oars of Eric's long-ship dip into the water, and, at his signal, his four oarsmen followed suit. When they had drawn clear of the headland, both ships turned south and raised their sails. By his side, Olaf tugged at the rudder until his ship's bow followed in the wake of the long-ship. When Madog finally looked back, the beach had already passed from view. The search for a new world was underway, equipped with two ships, crewed by sixty-eight men and one boy, or so Madog thought.

8

Madog settled himself on the rock ledge and leaned back into a small patch of shade. The smell of smoke, roasting meat and fish hung heavily in the air, and he wondered how much longer the work below would take. Grouped around a number of fires, Eric's men were busily smoking and salting the food. Further along the beach, Rhodri and some of the others were fishing with hand-lines. Although novices to the art, the fish were so abundant that almost every throw of the line was rewarded with a catch. Madog prayed that when the day came to eat these provisions, the sea would be kinder than it had been during their voyage down the coast of France. The memory of the ship's non-stop rolling and pitching still made him cringe. Even the Norsemen, with all their experience of the sea, had suffered with seasickness. It was not until they were nearing Portugal that the sea resumed its steady rolling motion.

His thoughts followed the route on which Eric had insisted. Sailing south, they had passed the last landmark of Europe, the coastline turning eastward at this point. Eric had hailed the *Moel-y-Gest* and, pointing east, had called out the name of Italy. Madog had heard of that country and guessed that the coast led to the great inland sea that lapped the shores of the Holy Land. Ahead of them, a range of high mountains beckoned and, as the ships drew nearer, the travellers could see that, despite the warmth, their peaks were snow-capped.

Keeping on the same heading, they had followed the rugged coast for four days. Here and there, they had seen small villages, and had stopped at one to obtain fresh water. The natives, who were dressed in long flowing robes, had eyed their visitors with some suspicion until Eric held out a gold coin, when their dark eyes had gleamed with pleasure. They had led the way to a deep well and when all the leather bags had been filled, they offered dates to the travellers. Further to the south, the cliffs changed to steep sand dunes, which ran on endlessly. After a night spent ashore, Madog had climbed to the top of the nearest dune. Behind him lay the deep blue sea, while to his front, golden sand hills ran eastward as far as the eye could see. He had been awed by the vast emptiness of the land and was glad to rejoin his companions below.

Eric had led them even further south until, one morning, he gave a ringing whoop of joy. The long-ship immediately turned west and as the *Moel-y-Gest* followed, Madog saw its sail billow out from a following breeze. Aided by this new, warm wind, both ships picked up speed and, before long, the coast of North Africa faded into the distance. They held this course for three days, and on the morning of the fourth, a cone-shaped object appeared on the horizon. The Norse ship's bow swung around until it pointed directly at the cone, which slowly grew higher as they sailed on. It was well past noon before the travellers could see that their goal was a very high mountain, which Madog later learned was a volcano. They landed on a stretch of fine, black sand, which led up to steep slopes covered with lush vegetation, while sparkling streams cascaded down. Several buildings, which appeared to be farms, stood balanced on the slopes, each one surrounded by terraced gardens.

'Truly, the Garden of Eden,' Cynon had exclaimed, as the men refilled the few emptied water bags. Later, Madog had joined some of his companions, who were swimming in the clear sea. The sun burned his white skin as he plunged in, and he had laughed with pleasure at the water's warmth. A cry of warning brought the swimmers quickly back to the beach and, seeing the cause, every man hastily armed himself. With levelled spears and marching in two ranks, some one hundred men were advancing toward the ships. Welsh and Norse drew close together and waited until the two ranks halted a short distance from them. For a while, the two groups studied each other in silence. The natives were dressed in the strangest of costume; they were wearing kilts, and sleeveless tunics made from a fine, white cloth. A strip of the same material was bound around each man's head and was adorned with a number of white feathers, while their feet were protected by soft, untanned leather. Yet the strangest of all was the fact that these men, though burned by the sun, were unquestionably white. They were tall, blue-eyed, and their shoulder length hair was blonde.

'Not unlike Eric and most of his Norsemen,' Madog had thought. He had felt Rhodri touch his shoulder.

'Will you look at their weapons,' the soldier had whispered. 'There is not a trace of metal on any spear.'

Madog saw that this was, indeed, the truth. The spears had tips made of sharp stone, or were simply sharpened to a point. Suddenly, one of the islanders stepped forward and spoke out in a commanding tone. His speech was unlike any other that the travellers had heard, and they stared blankly at him. When he had stopped talking, another silence followed, and Madog decided to try to break the impasse. He moved forward a pace and waved a hand at those behind him.

'Welshmen, Norsemen,' he said loudly, and then, pointing to himself, he added, 'Madog.'

The imposing native nodded his understanding and, indicating his followers, called out, 'Guanches,' then, patting his chest, he said, 'Caichta.'

He eyed the traveller's weapons and seemed to come to a decision. At his command, the islanders had lowered their spears and watched as their chief waded into the water and examined the long-ship. Madog could see that the man was fascinated by the nails that held the planks together, and saw him shake his head in wonder. His examination completed, Caichta rejoined his men and, as he did so, Eric walked boldly up to him. Miming the act of eating, the Norse leader had held out a coin and offered it to the chief. Caichta had peered at the coin, then, with a shrug, had given it back. Not to be outdone, Eric had taken a knife from his belt and held it out. The chief had made to take the weapon, but Eric had stepped back, repeating the mime, his message clear to everyone. Thus, the islanders brought food to the travellers: plump fowls, small, fat pigs, and an abundance of strange fruits.

Madog's memories came to a sudden stop when a group of islanders appeared at the far end of the beach. In the lead was Caichta, and his purposeful walk brought Madog to his feet. As he made his way down to the black sand, he saw Tudor and Jean running beside the water's edge. He smiled as he remembered the surprise appearance of Tudor, when the lad had dashed from the storeroom to hang over the ship's side. It had been late on the second day of their voyage that the stowaway had been forced to come onto the deck, when it was too late to turn back and return him to his parents. Since then, the two boys had become inseparable.

'Something is about to happen, Madog,' Eric said, when the young man joined him. 'I fancy our stay here is about to end.'

He was right. When Caichta came to a halt in front of them, he held out a hand and gestured that he now wanted Eric's knife. The Norseman nodded and handed the weapon to the chief, who held it high for all to see. His next move was equally plain. Pointing towards the sun, he raised one finger then swept his arm seawards. His meaning was plain: on the morrow, his visitors must leave the island.

'It would seem that we are no longer welcome,' Eric said, as they watched the islanders march away. 'However, it is of no matter. We have all the food and water that we can carry.'

He began to walk towards the long-ship then, turning back, he gripped Madog's shoulder, 'It's west once more,' he said excitedly. 'This could be easier than I had hoped. We found this island, so maybe we will find more out there.'

Sunrise on the following day found the two ships already at sea. On the *Moel-y-Gest*, Madog watched the long-ship's oars break into their steady rhythm. He was aware that the Norsemen could leave him astern at will, and gave a cry of satisfaction, when his ship's sail filled with the following breeze. The tip of the volcano on the island of Tenerife could still be seen on the second day out, finally sinking below the horizon as dusk fell. The traveller's last link with the Old World had gone.

Jean held the stick firmly as Tudor cut another notch into it. A shower of spray swept over them and caused both lads to move quickly under the cover of the upper deck. 'How many days has it been now?' Jean asked, as he grabbed a beam to steady himself.

'One more than yesterday,' Tudor answered sarcastically, then, seeing the hurt look on his friend's face, he added, 'Twenty-eight days and twenty-seven nights. We must be close to the edge of the world by now, that is, if it is really out here. I do wish this wind would ease so that we could climb back up the mast.'

Jean nodded his agreement. Down here on the lower deck, all they could see were the passing waves. He looked upwards to where Madog stood clutching the upper deck rail. Their captain had forbidden the two lads to take their usual post as lookouts, when the squall had hit, and Jean knew that Madog was right. Anyone falling into these wild waves would be lost forever.

His legs braced apart, Madog felt the stern rise beneath

him. By now, he scarcely noticed the ship's motion in normal weather, and he found the squall exhilarating. It was almost a month since they had left Tenerife, and scarcely a day had passed when this following wind had not blown. On most days, there was no more than a light breeze; other days were like today. Madog pulled his cloak tighter as the next wave passed beneath the ship, sending spray high into the air, and he turned to look at the men on the rudder. Olaf and Torberg, two of the four Norsemen on board, grinned back at him, obviously enjoying the squall as much as he was.

The sail of the *Moel-y-Gest* had been partly lowered so that, on the crest of every wave, he caught a glimpse of the long-ship just ahead. Eric's men had brought their oars in-board, showing up their ship's sleek lines. What the conditions on board were like, Madog could only guess at, for the lighter ship tended to corkscrew back into the trough between two waves. He caught a brief glimpse of Eric, and gave an answering wave of his arm, before his friend ducked under cover.

The squall ended as quickly as it had started. One moment the wind was howling over the ships, the next it had gone. For a while longer, the sea seethed around them, then, gradually, it eased once more and assumed a steady rolling motion. It was well past noon by now. Madog climbed down to the lower deck and called to the Breton, Raoul, to join him. Between them, they sliced up a salted joint of meat, which they shared amongst the crew. When it came to Jean's turn to be served with food, the Breton fondly ruffled the lad's fair hair, and father and son smiled at each other. Madog noticed this exchange of affection and congratulated himself on having saved Raoul's life. The Breton had turned out to be an excellent sailor, always willing to work at any task, and he even seemed to enjoy his spell on the oars.

With the meat shared out, water was the next commodity.

For the past few days, Madog had ordered that the precious drink had to be strictly rationed. Almost a half of the leather bags were now empty. With no idea how long it would be before they sighted land, he deemed this precaution vital. Whenever it had rained, the crew had collected as much water as they were able to, but the result of their efforts was soon used up. The thought of what would happen should they run out of water sprang to Madog's mind and he quickly put it aside. Later, as the sun lowered in the sky, the *Moel-y-Gest* drew closer to the long-ship, and the crews used a rope to link both vessels together, ensuring that they stayed close during the night. Two men were posted as watch, while the remainder drew together on the lower deck and made ready for sleep. Another day on the Atlantic came to a close.

Seven more days passed. By now, even the most apprehensive members of the two crews began to doubt that the edge of the world lay in their path. Wherever it was, it became increasingly unlikely that it was in this vast expanse of sea. Two days before, there had been a cry of delight from the masthead. All eyes had, looked up at the two lads, clinging to the masthead, who were pointing to starboard. At their shouts of 'birds', everyone had rushed to that side of the ship, to see that this was indeed true. Skimming the water, a flock of bright blue birds was flying directly at then. Amidst cries of dismay from the crew, several of the creatures dropped into the sea, only to re-appear, magically, within moments. The dumbfounded men watched as the flock parted, to pass the ship. Only as the last of the birds drew near did this wonder explain itself. There were several thumps on the deck, and what everyone had thought were birds revealed themselves to be fish.

'Fish that can fly,' Cynon had remarked. 'Now I have truly seen everything.' Apart from this strange event, one day was much like the last, though today was different. For the first time since leaving Tenerife, there had been no wind. The sea still had a gentle swell, yet the ship's sail hung limply and the *Moel-y-Gest* was being towed by the long-ship. Madog had taken his turn on the oars and had rowed until the chaffing on his hands had forced him to stop. Later that night, he took the first watch with Raoul, their surroundings filling him with content. An immense moon was rising behind them, lighting the white foam crests of the gentle waves, while casting shadows between each swell. Although Madog had seen the moon on many nights, its size this far south still surprised him. With no wind, the only sounds were the gentle hiss of the passing waves and the creaking timbers of the *Moel-y-Gest*. Ahead of him, the long-ship rose and dipped in the sea's gentle swell. It was, indeed, a perfect night. Then, in the blink of an eye, the scene changed. Loud cries of alarm came from the long-ship and, to his horror, Madog saw the craft tip sideways. For a sickening few moments, he thought that it was about to turn over, and then, somehow, the Norse ship righted itself. The next moment, the sea exploded around the two ships and huge shapes moved swiftly through the water. Madog felt the *Moel-y-Gest* rock violently beneath him as something passed by the bow. Awestruck, he saw a huge tail, almost the size of the ship, rise in the air. With a deafening crash, the tail came down into the sea, drenching all aboard, and then a massive creature slid beneath the waves.

When the sea finally settled, Madog and some of the crew hauled on the towrope until they drew alongside the long-ship. Eric's men were just hauling aboard the last of the four men who had been pitched into the sea. For a while, no-one spoke, as each man recovered from his fright. It was Eric, standing at the stern of his long-ship, who broke the silence. The big man threw back his head and began to laugh, a reaction that was soon taken up by everyone. Their encounter with a family of sleeping whales would be an experience that no man there would ever forget.

'Well, Madog, what do you think of our situation now?' Cynon asked, joining the young man at the stern rail. 'There is still no sign of land, after all these days at sea. I had prayed my thanks to God, when I first saw those fish that we thought were birds. They made me believe for a brief moment that our travels were soon to end.'

'I only wish I could say some words of encouragement to you,' Madog answered.' I honestly do not know what to think any more. We may find land on the morrow, or we may never find it at all. I try hard not to ponder about that prospect. One thing I am clear about, though, is the fact that we do not have enough provisions to survive turning back.'

Cynon grunted, then gave a slight shiver.

'The day feels cooler to me, though the sun shines brightly. I must go and put my cloak on. I fear a man's blood turns thinner as he gets older.'

Madog watched the old man climb carefully down to the lower deck. What Cynon had said was quite true; there was a noticeable chill in the air. He leaned over the rail and saw a score or more of large jellyfish drifting by, their pink bodies trailing behind them. He watched them for a few moments, and had just looked up at the masthead, when a cry from Tudor rang out. The lad was pointing out to sea and, as Madog turned in that direction, a large dorsal fin broke the surface and moved closer. There was something sinister about the fin and, as it drew opposite to where he stood, a head briefly surfaced. The wide mouth opened in what seemed to be an evil smile, and Madog stepped back from the rail at the sight of rows of razor sharp teeth. With a powerful flick of its tail, the shark moved on.

'Not a creature to share the water with,' Madog thought with a shudder.

A shout from the long-ship caught his attention and he saw that its crew had drawn their oars in-board. Slowly, the *Moel-y-Gest* drew alongside, and a rope, passed over from the Norse ship, was made secure.

'We need more food and water,' Eric called out, as the two ships drew together. 'I do not care for this coldness in the air. It is a sure sign of a storm. I think that we should divide the provisions, in case we get separated.'

He looked eastward and frowned with concern, and Madog turned to see for himself. Covering the whole width of the horizon was an enormous black cloud, heading towards them. At Eric's urging, his crew hurried with their task of loading the food and water. While this was going on, he spoke with Olaf and Torberg in Norse and then with Madog.

'I have told them to keep sailing west,' he said. 'We must do everything possible to keep in sight of each other.' He saw the worried look on Madog's face, and added, 'Trust in my Norsemen, my friend. You have four of my best seamen on board.'

He gave Madog a brief smile of encouragement, and turned his attention towards his crew. Madog caught a brief glimpse of Elise and Rhodri, and gave them a wave. Both men raised an arm in return, and he was pleased to see that they both looked well.

When the task was completed, the rope was released and the two ships began to drift apart. By now, white caps were showing on the waves and a wind began to howl around the *Moel-y-Gest*. His men were frantically tying down anything that moved, including the furled sail. He saw that Olaf and Torberg were busy lashing themselves to the rudder. Both men kept glancing astern and, with a twinge of fear, Madog saw the rapidly approaching blackness. He suddenly felt the ship heave beneath him, though the waves were normal. It was as though a giant, unseen hand was playing with the craft. He searched and found a length of rope, and yelled to those below to secure themselves as best they could. He saw that Cynon, Raoul and the two lads were sitting at the foot of the mast. Again, the ship heaved, as he staggered towards the two Norsemen, and tied himself to the rail next to them.

The sound of the wind became deafening, making his head ring. He risked a glance astern and, as he did so, a sheet of rain struck him in the face. A moment later, the full force of the storm hit the ship, enveloping the *Moel-y-Gest* in a fearsome grey world. The noise of the wind deadened every other sound, and half blinded, by the stinging rain, Madog saw that the long-ship was already hidden from sight. Again, the stern began to lift, and he saw the Norsemen's feet leave the deck as the rudder cleared the water. With a sickening crash, the ship dropped back down, and Madog threw himself onto the rudder, adding his strength to that of the other two men. Whatever happened, they must keep the wind behind them. Should the ship turn sideways on, the *Moel-y-Gest* would capsize.

Through slitted eyes, Madog saw Olaf look astern and then shout to him, his voice snatched away by the wind. Still wrestling with the rudder, he looked back, his mouth opening in awe at what he saw. A wall of water at least twenty feet high was overtaking the ship, and the stern lifted skywards. The next moment, the huge wave broke over the ship, blotting out everything else. Green water boiled over him, and he was swept off his feet, his lifeline jerking him painfully to a stop. The sea passed over him and, gasping for air, he saw the ship's bow disappear under the crushing wave. For a few terrifying moments, he thought that the *Moel-y-Gest* was about to plunge into the depths. Then, miraculously, the bow slowly lifted. Giving thanks to the Almighty and the skills of the ship's builders, he turned his attention to the lower deck.

The scene below was one of utter chaos. Swirling around in the receding water were barrels of salted meat, torn planks of wood and rope. Yet, far worse was the sight of the crew. Despite their lifelines, most of them had been flung into a heap toward the bow, while several lay senseless. Madog saw Tudor and Jean grab hold of one and turn him face upwards. The man struggled feebly to his knees and pulled himself to the mast, where he sat by Cynon. The old man waved weakly up at Madog, who returned to his battle with the rudder.

The storm blew relentlessly, numbing the minds of everyone aboard. Their initial feeling of fear gave way to one of resignation as the *Moel-y-Gest* was tossed like a piece of flotsam on the raging sea. Madog had no idea where the long-ship was. Occasionally, there would be a brief lifting of the greyness, but the sea remained empty. The day wore on; he felt his strength failing, and he became aware that Torberg and Olaf were in the same state. One thing became increasingly clear to his tired mind: the three of them would soon be unable to control the rudder, and no man aboard could possibly come to their aid. When that moment came, the ship would founder.

A sense of despair swept over Madog as he peered at the racing seas that surrounded the *Moel-y-Gest*. Every muscle in his body had become an agony, and he knew that he had reached the limit of his endurance. Another break in the driving rain came and, without hope, he looked ahead of the ship. For a few moments, he thought that he was deluding himself and he wiped the rain from his eyes with a free hand. The illusion was still there when he looked again. Unable to believe his eyes, Madog grabbed Torberg's shoulder and pointed. The Norseman squinted ahead, shook his head and looked again. Madog faintly heard his cry of amazement and knew, then, that what he had seen was a reality. Dead ahead of the *Moel-y-Gest* was a line of windswept trees.

Until then, he had had no idea of how fast the ship had been moving. He had been aware only of the driven rain and waves sweeping past. Now, however, he could see that they were approaching the tree line at speed. In vain, he yelled a warning to those below, then braced himself. The wait was a short one. Some fifty paces from the shore, the *Moel-y-Gest* gave an almost human scream of pain and keeled over onto its side.

The three men on the rudder were thrown down the now vertical deck, until their life lines brought them to a painful stop. For a while, they dangled helplessly above the raging water, and Madog saw some of the crew clinging to the mast, which had snapped off. He felt a hand on his arm and saw Olaf beside him. The Norseman held a knife and, yelling an unheard warning, he cut Madog's line. Madog shot down the deck, thumped into the submerged rail and went under water. The sea spun him around like a top, threatening to suck him down and, frantically, he kicked for the surface. As his head broke clear and he gulped air into his lungs, something struck him a stunning blow and everything faded away. He was vaguely aware of hands grabbing him and lifting him half out of the water. Gradually, his senses began to clear and he found that he was lying over the mast, with Raoul's arm holding him firm. Around him, men were struggling for their lives as they tried to reach the mast. With horror, he saw one man throw up his arms and sink beneath the surface.

A speeding wave lifted the shattered mast clear of the wreckage and strangely, gracefully deposited the heavy timber on a narrow strip of sand. Madog felt the land's firmness beneath his feet; and, with the last of his remaining strength, he staggered ashore. Half-drowned, half-conscious, he slumped to his knees. His journey to the New World had finally ended.

9

Madog and the two lads slithered through the mud and peered anxiously into the eerie mangrove swamp. The storm had passed on shortly after dawn, leaving a clear, blue sky and a calm sea behind it. With the coming of daylight, the shipwrecked crew had gathered on the beach, arriving in twos and threes, delighted to find that others had survived. Yet, after a while, it became clear that not all of them had been so lucky. Three of their comrades were missing. One of Rhodri's men, one of the young fishermen and Cynon had failed to show up. Sickened with worry, Madog had pleaded with the exhausted men to help him search along the shore, which they had agreed to do, although their efforts had been in vain, and most of them had returned to where the Moel-y-Gest lay in its final resting place. Only Tudor and Jean continued the search with Madog.

'Have you no idea what happened to Cynon?' Madog asked Tudor, as they moved carefully toward the base of the next tree.

'None at all,' Tudor answered. 'The last we saw of him was when he cut our lifelines. He was all right then. When Jean's father pulled us up onto the mast, I looked around, but there was no trace of him. The only other person we saw was you.'

The three stopped to rest on the roots of the tree, and looked around them again. The swamp really was a creepy place. The foliage of the trees almost cut off the sunlight, while the tangled roots formed weird shapes that stood as high as a man. Everywhere was the constant humming of insects and an over-powering stench of rotting vegetation, but by far the worst was the suffocating heat, which seemed to suck the air from their lungs.

'Will you two come a little further with me?' Madog asked, aware that both lads were as tired as he was. Tudor leaned over and picked up a long, stout stick from the mud. He nodded.

'A little further, Madog,' he answered wearily. 'Not too far, I beg you; else you will have to carry me out of this horrid place.'

Tudor looked at Jean, who was staring fearfully about him.

'What about you, Jean? Would you rather rest here while we look further?' he asked.

Jean shook his head vigorously.' I'm not staying here on my own,' he answered.' My legs feel like lead, and yet, I will crawl if needs be.'

In single file, with Madog taking the lead, the three resumed their search, calling out every now and then. The only response to their cries, however, was the screech and chatter from the many brightly coloured birds high up in the treetops. The further they went, the more convinced Madog became that Cynon had not made the safety of the beach, and a feeling of guilt began to take hold of him. If he had not embarked on this madcap idea, the old man would have been living contentedly back in Brittany. With this on his mind, he scarcely noticed the large pool that barred their path. Without thinking, he stepped onto a partly submerged log and instinctively knew that he had made a terrible mistake. The log shot forward and a rock-hard tail swung violently through the air and knocked him flat. Winded by the blow, Madog lay helpless in the shallow water and watched in horror as the creature turned towards him. Yellow eyes glared from a green-scaled head; and as the alligator slid toward him, he saw the huge jaws open to reveal its teeth. Desperately, Madog bent his legs and pushed himself away from the oncoming creature. He felt hands tugging him backwards and then saw

Tudor dash forward and thrust his stick into the gaping mouth. The jaws snapped shut with a loud crack, splintering the wood into pieces. For a few moments, the alligator shook its head, as it tried to dislodge the fragments from its jaws. That action saved Madog's life. With Jean's help, he regained his feet. After ensuring that Tudor had rejoined them, he turned and ran.

Their search through the swamp had run roughly parallel to the sea, and the three now made towards it. Gasping for air, they forced their aching limbs to move ever faster and, before long, they burst out of the swamp and into the open. Here, a low bank of fine sand barred their way. Without pause, the three scrambled over it and reached the safety of the beach. After a few more agonising paces, Madog led the way into the cooling sea, where they lay, exhausted by their flight. Gradually his heart ceased its wild pounding and he began to wash the swamp's filth from his body. The two lads did likewise and felt the water slowly revive them. All the while, one or the other would look back toward the swamp, but they were happy to note that there was no sign of the alligator.

Eventually, Madog got to his feet.

'Come, lads, we had best return to the others ,' he said. 'My thanks to you both for saving me, back there. It was a brave thing you did, facing up to that monster. Many a man would have fled.'

The two boys shuffled their feet in embarrassment and, to save them from this, Madog led off along the beach.

On their return to the *Moel-y-Gest*, they found that the others were inspecting the wrecked ship. The tide had ebbed and Madog could now see what had happened during the storm. A large tree stump with a mass of twisted roots protruded above the surface of the water; it held the capsized ship in a vice-like grip. A hole some three feet wide had been torn in the hull and it extended almost the full length of the ship, and Madog knew instantly that there was no hope of repairing such damage. He heard his name being called and saw Raoul wading through the waist deep water and beckoning to him.

'Some good news, at least,' the Breton called. 'Much of our drinking-water is safe and some of the food. Come and see for yourself.'

Two of the others helped Madog aboard. By passing from one dangling line to the next, he followed Raoul to the storeroom, where the four Norsemen were gathering the leather water bags, which had been suspended from hooks in the beams. Olaf grinned a welcome and thrust one of them into Madog's hands. Cautiously, he opened the neck of the bag, raised it to his lips and sipped its contents. The cool liquid tasted like nectar and washed the taste of salt from his mouth.

'The Saints be praised. This is surely the sweetest drink of my life,' he exclaimed, after taking a mouthful. 'What of the food?'

'The sea has ruined much of it,' Raoul answered. 'Some of it has remained above the water's level and we are sure that it is safe to eat.'

On Madog's suggestion, the men formed a line and passed the stores from one man to another, until all was safely deposited on the beach. At first, most of them were wary of eating, but as they watched the bolder of their comrades chew on the meat, they gave way to their hunger.

'We should go hunting in the swamp,' one of the men suggested. 'I, for one, could do with the taste of freshly-cooked meat.'

Madog saw the two lads look at him, and he related their narrow escape from the alligator. The men heard his tale in silence, and there was no more talk of entering the swamp. When everyone had eaten and had drunk a little water, there was a general movement back to the ship. On his return, each man carried a sword or knife, which they had managed to salvage. On the fisherman's advice, the weapons were first dried in the sun and then burnished with handfuls of fine sand. With dusk approaching and the alligator in mind, Madog suggested that they should build a ring of fires. Dead timber was plentiful along the beach and, after a few attempts, some of the men succeeded in getting a spark from their tinderboxes. Between them, they made up a rota of guards to keep watch and fuel the fires and, as night fell, the majority settled down to sleep.

Before he joined them, Madog took one more look around him. Despite their predicament, the firelight made the scene somehow cheerful and the movement of the men on guard brought a sense of security. He thought again of Cynon. That the old man had died in the storm was now beyond question. Again, he felt guilt begin to take him over, but then he remembered Cynon's determination to accompany him, when they had walked through the wood in Brittany. It had been the old man's decision, yet whether Madog could have stopped him, he would never know. What he did know was that he had lost his strongest link with the past.

The survivors of the *Moel-y-Gest* greeted the dawn with relief. Exhausted by their ordeal, the sleep that they craved had been denied them. No sooner had they settled down to rest on the night before, than clouds of white insects, attracted by the firelight, descended on them. The peace of the night was soon shattered as the men slapped at the biting mosquitoes and, cursing with rage, had plunged into the sea for relief. The choice between alligators or insects was difficult to make, though, in the end, several of the fires were dampened down with seaweed. Only by crouching over the reeking smoke could a man find some escape from his tormentors. When daylight finally arrived, the men had looked at each other in disbelief. All had suffered numerous bites, and now their faces and exposed limbs were so puffed up that friends had difficulty recognising each other. The thought of spending another night on this beach was too much for Madog and he called the men together.

'Are we agreed that we make a move?' he asked first.

The men growled their assent.

'The sooner the better, I say,' one of them called out, 'but which way do we go; north or south?'

'I have been thinking hard about this,' Madog answered. 'The last we saw of the long-ship, it was to our port side, which I believe would mean that Eric reached land further to our south. I think that we should go in that direction, which would give us a greater chance of meeting up with him.'

'That is, if they survived the storm,' another man added. 'What if they all perished?'

'Then we must pray that they did not,' Madog answered curtly. 'Anyway, I am not staying here a moment longer, so let us be on our way.'

After ensuring that they had not overlooked any weapon or water bag, the men formed into line and began to walk south. Madog did not hurry them and set an easy pace, keeping close to the water's edge, where the sand was firmer under foot. The sun was high in the sky when he called a halt and they moved to the fringe of the swamp to seek shade. Mindful of the alligator, two of the men kept watch, peering into the gloomy swamp while their comrades dozed. Tudor and Jean, though, were still full of life and together waded into the clear water to swim. The sea eased their aches and, despite its salt stinging their bites, both lads floated blissfully on their backs for a while. Finally deciding that they had enough, they waded ashore and as they stepped onto the hot, dry sand, Jean gripped his companion's arm tightly. Tudor winced as Jean's fingers tightened even more, and he turned angrily to remonstrate with the younger lad. Jean's face was a picture of disbelief, and with his free hand the young Breton pointed south and out to sea. Heading towards them, its oars rising and falling in steady rhythm, was the unmistakable shape of the long-ship.

Their loud whoops of joy brought every man scrambling to his feet and, in moments, they stood in a group at the water's edge. Madog's relief on sighting the ship knew no bounds. A tremendous weight lifted from his young shoulders and, unashamedly, he let his tears of joy run down his cheeks. The men's cries carried over the water, and they saw the oars quicken their beat, the wolf's head swinging around until it pointed directly towards them.

With a loud crunching sound, the long-ship's bow ploughed over the sand and came to a stop. Those aboard leapt ashore, shouting joyfully at their friends, and the beach quickly became a scene of wild reunion. Madog happily let Eric sweep him off his feet and whirl him around, before Rhodri caught him in a crushing embrace,

'By the Saints, I feared that we had lost you,' the big man shouted. 'The last glimpse we had of you was moments before that huge wave struck us. After that, the sea remained empty except for us.'

He released his hold and ruffled Madog's hair.

'I have been worried about you, lad,' he said gruffly. 'I must admit that I gave a heartfelt prayer of thanks when I saw you on the beach just now.' He looked closely at Madog and then whistled in surprise and asked, 'What has happened to your face? You look as though you have been in a fist fight.'

'Insects, millions of insects,' Madog answered. 'We were tormented by them all night; but what of you? You are only a shadow of your normal self.'

'Rowing on a belly only half full of fish,' the soldier snorted. 'I could kill for a meal of sweet lamb or venison.' He looked around the gathering and the smile left his lips. 'Where is Cynon? Is he resting somewhere?' he asked.

'I fear that Cynon was lost when we capsized,' Madog answered softly. 'We searched for him and two others, but to no avail. Their resting place is somewhere out at sea.'

Rhodri remained silent for a while, looking out over the water. 'I shall miss the old man,' he said finally. 'I know my drinking annoyed him and much of it was done only to tease him. Yet, with a word or a look, he could make me feel like some naughty child.'

At this point, they were rejoined by Eric, who had been talking with Olaf and the other Norsemen.

'I must speak with you, Madog,' he said. 'There is too much chatter here. Come, walk with me.'

Side by side, they followed the water's edge for a while, until Eric came to a halt.

'My men tell me that your ship is a total wreck,' he said. 'Your crew will be a welcome addition to the long-ship. We can really use its speed, with the extra hands.' He stared across the sand towards the swamp, and a look of despondency swept over his face.

'This place is not what I was hoping to find,' he said sadly. 'It is indeed a Godforsaken land. We landed at a place many miles from here and the swamp was also there.' He looked hard at Madog, then added, 'We have no choice but to sail on. I need to know if you agree to come with us.'

'As you say, we have no choice,' Madog replied. 'I will be glad to be away from here, and I know the others feel the same.'

Together, they rejoined the men and told them of their decision.

'The sooner we move away from here the better,' several of them called out. 'Anywhere has got to be better than this.'

The men pushed the long-ship out into the water and, in a short while, everyone was aboard. Oars were secured in their locks and, at Eric's command, the men took the strain and the craft began to slip smoothly through the sea.

10

The noon sun beat down on the drifting longboat. It had now become routine to lower the big sail as the sun climbed in the sky, and rig it over the crew, to provide shade. The heat sapped a man's strength, and Eric wisely ordered the oars shipped aboard as noon approached. For the moment, drinking water was not a worry. The leather bags had been refilled two days previously, yet everyone drank sparingly, not knowing when they might find another spring ashore. Madog and some of the men were seated together, each man lost in his own thoughts.

'Were it not for this heat, I would have been in favour of staying at that last landing place,' Rhodri said, breaking the silence. 'It was a pretty enough place.' 'That's true,' Madog replied with a smile, 'though, no doubt, the venison had something to do with you liking it so much.'

'That meat saved my life, I can tell you,' Rhodri said, smacking his lips. 'I thank the Almighty for sending us those fine deer.'

'I think it's Elise you should thank,' one of the others remarked. 'Without his bowmen's skill, we would never have brought them down.'

Madog thought back to the scene when they had landed. While Eric and a few of the men guarded the long-ship, he had led a party in search of water. They had scarcely lost sight of the craft, when they discovered a stream of clear running water. It was not the stream, however, that had sent the men rushing forward, but the sight of a herd of small deer drinking from it. The startled animals wheeled around, and bolted in every direction, and only then did Elise and his bowmen loose their arrows.

'It could well be your last meat for a while, Rhodri,' Elise said, holding up his bow. 'I doubt this string will shoot many more arrows. The sea water has sapped its strength.'

'What of the bow staff?' Madog asked.

'That is well enough,' Elise answered. 'We have always kept the wood greased, to protect it.'

''Tis a strange land, this New World,' one of the others said, changing the subject. 'There are miles and miles of swamp, and then some stretches of fine, rolling country. If it were cooler, a man could settle here.'

'You would be on your own,' Rhodri remarked. 'Our Norse friends do not like this heat, and I feel the same about it.'

'That's true enough,' a bowman named Tomas agreed. 'I begin to sweat, the moment I go ashore. There must be something in the air, I fear.'

They fell silent again, and Madog allowed his mind to wander. Twenty days had passed since they had joined up again with the long-ship. At first, they had sailed south, then west, and then, they followed the coastline north. Finally, they had turned west once more. The Norsemen all agreed that they had sailed around a large tract of land that jutted out into the sea.

'A peninsula, it was, not unlike your Lleyn, only much bigger,' Eric had told him, when he described it.

Ahead of them now, they could see that the shore swung southward again, and Madog resigned himself to more swampland and heat. One by one, those around him closed their eyes; Madog made himself comfortable and did the same.

He awoke to the sounds of voices arguing loudly, and looked in the direction of the commotion. He saw that Eric and some of his men were gathered at the bow, all of them gazing intently towards land. His curiosity aroused, Madog picked his way among the reclining figures and joined them.

'What is amiss?' he asked.

Eric turned a puzzled face toward him.

'The tides have gone mad,' he answered. 'We should be between ebb and flood now, but we are being pushed further out to sea. I cannot understand it, Madog. The only explanation is that there are three tides in one day and night in this part of the world, not two as everywhere else. Old Torberg, of course, thinks differently.'

Madog looked at the grizzled Norseman who was leaning over the side of the ship and staring into the water.

'What does he think is happening?' he asked.

Eric was about to explain when Torberg gave a cry of triumph. At his bidding, a baling pail and a length of rope were passed to him. In moments, he had dropped the pail overboard and quickly pulled it back. He cupped his free hand into the pail, scooped up a handful of the water and put it to his lips. The others watched in silence as Torberg swished the water around his mouth, before spitting it out over the side.

'I'm right,' he told Eric. 'Much of this is fresh water. It tastes muddy, I admit, but it's fresh water, all the same. We are being taken along by a river emptying into the sea, Eric. It must be a huge one, to be so powerful.'

Eric told Madog, in his broken Welsh, what the old Norseman had said.

'Are you willing to find out for sure?' he asked. 'This could be a passage inland. Should there be more swamps, we can always return here and try further west.'

Madog agreed without hesitation. He had had enough of the cramped conditions on the long-ship and yearned to stretch his legs on land. 'Preferably dry land' he thought. At Eric's command, the oars were put out; men took their places and, in unison, began to row. The long-ship responded as though it were a willing partner, its bow cleaving through the calm sea, the wolf's head pointing toward the shore. When their speed had built up, the oarsmen settled into a steady rhythm and, after a while, they could make out a tree line. Then, what appeared to be a wide gap appeared, slightly to port, and Eric steered the craft towards its centre. A feeling of excitement took hold of those aboard as the long-ship eventually entered the gap. It was at least two miles wide, its banks made up of dried mud, before the trees took over.

The current immediately grew stronger, and now the crew began to strain on their oars to keep up speed. The further they went, the narrower the channel became, until it measured less than a mile between its banks.

Despite all their effort, the long-ship began to slow and, mindful that the men were far from fit, Eric steered towards the right bank. Here, two of the men took a line ashore and secured it to a waterlogged tree stump.

'Rest for now, lads,' he called out. 'We will wait here for the tide. We might as well let Mother Nature help us.'

The sun was lowering in the sky when the water level began to rise, although Eric waited awhile before ordering the line to be cast off. Aided by the incoming sea, the long-ship once again moved swiftly through the water, the oarsmen watching the riverbank slip by.

Quite suddenly, they came out into another channel, and as they moved out to its centre, the crew could see that they had travelled up a branch of a vast delta. However, it was what lay directly ahead that caught their attention. Flanked by more mud banks lay the mouth of a wide river, so wide that no man aboard had seen its like.

'Our passage inland,' Eric called out joyously. 'By its size, I would wager it must run for hundreds of miles.'

The men responded by straining harder on the oars, and the long-ship moved even faster as it entered the Mississippi river.

They had been twenty days on the river, the mud banks were behind them, replaced by trees and grassland. The further north they travelled, the sweeter the air became, its humidity lessening each day. The change transformed the men, their lethargy diminishing with every passing day. This and a steady supply of meat and wild berries, which they craved, worked wonders.

'You are putting weight back on,' Madog remarked to Rhodri. 'You look more your old self.'

'Aye, lad, and glad of it, I can tell you,' the soldier replied. 'I doubt that my arms would have had the strength to wield my sword, and were it not for the rowing, most of us would have been useless in combat.'

'There is not much fear of that happening,' Madog said. 'Those few natives we met are hardly likely to cause us any trouble.'

Two days ago, he had led a hunting party inland. Breaking clear of the tree line, they had walked straight into a small band of natives. Both groups were startled by the encounter, and before Madog could give some sign of friendship, the natives had bolted.

'It is little wonder that they ran,' he said with a laugh. 'Our appearance would frighten anyone.'

'You have never spoken truer,' Rhodri replied, joining in the mirth. 'We do look like a bunch of wild men. There is no question that we shall have to dress ourselves in deer skins before long.'

The two studied their comrades and laughed the louder. Each man, including the Welsh, was bearded, his hair long and straggly, his clothing in tatters.

'Deerskin is what those natives were wearing,' Madog said, 'although there was only enough to cover what modesty demands. I would be happy to wear an animal's hide rather than be naked.'

The long-ship continued its journey up the river, the crew enjoying every moment. Only Elise and his bowmen were not content, for their bowstrings had finally frayed and snapped.

'I do not feel right without my trusty bow, Madog,' Elise had complained. 'Those natives back there carried small bows, and I would dearly like to know what they use for springing them.'

'No doubt we shall meet up with others before long,' Madog assured him. 'I am sure that we shall soon have another chance to show them that we mean no harm.' After this conversation, Elise had rejoined his men and Madog had smiled to himself because the bowman's use of his name in place of Sire had been a welcome surprise. Until now, Elise had been one of the few Welshmen still to use his title. It was something that pleased Madog, for out here, in the New World, they were all equal in status. Yet, strangely enough, despite his youth, he had noticed that, whenever a decision had to be made, the men looked to him for guidance.

Seven more days passed, their progress confirming the truth of Eric's belief that they were on a mighty river. It was on this day that they were forced to pull in to its western bank to discuss what lay ahead of them. They had now reached a point where the river split into two. Other rivers had flowed into the Mississippi, and they had ignored them, content to stay on the main stream. This time, though, it was different; there was little to choose between the two possible routes, other than that one continued northward, while the other turned west.

'Well, now, which is it to be?' Eric asked. 'Do we travel on north, or do we try a new direction?'

The men talked amongst themselves for a while and it soon became clear that they would never come to a decision.

'Why can we not stay here?' one of them called out. 'There is game in plenty and fish in the river.'

'True enough,' Eric agreed. 'Although, speaking for myself, I would like to see more of this country. Who knows what we may find. There must be native villages ahead for the people of these parts have to live somewhere.'

The men talked amongst themselves again and, with growing impatience, Madog got to his feet. He pointed to the eastern bank, which was thickly wooded, and then to the west, where rolling open grassland lay. The vast space seemed to beckon him, reminding him of the empty desert of Africa, where he had stood alone on its fringe.

'I'm for going west,' he declared boldly. 'The going looks easy enough, and the air is sweet with the fragrance of wild flowers, but above all, it's the thought of all that space in which to move freely.'

Eric translated Madog's words for the Norsemen, who only hesitated for a few moments before agreeing to the change in direction.

'We also agree, lad,' Rhodri said, speaking for the others. 'It would appear that there is little risk of us encountering any swampland out there.'

So it was that the long-ship and its crew sailed into the Missouri river.

The hunting party carefully raised their heads above the lip of the narrow streambed. They had spotted their prey some way off and had used the watercourse as concealment. Some fifty paces away, a herd of small deer grazed on the knee-high grass, unaware of the hunters' presence.

'Oh, what would I give for a newly strung bow,' Elise whispered into Madog's ear. 'A man could not wish for an easier shot.'

Madog nodded in agreement, and then signalled the others to spread out. By now, they were practiced in approaching these wily animals, and without a word, Tudor and Jean took their places at the ends of the line of men. They would have the furthest to run, using their speed to close the circle around their prey. At Madog's next signal, the two lads started over the lip and began to slide through the prairie grass, followed by the other hunters.

Slowly, carefully, they moved on their bellies toward the deer, until they guessed that that they had covered half the distance, when Madog cautiously raised his head. At that very moment, the herd ceased grazing and stared intently northward. For a few heartbeats, they stood motionless, and then suddenly sprang into flight. With a curse, Madog got to his feet and slid his sword into its scabbard. What had frightened the deer he did not know, though he was sure that it was not the hunters.

'What in the name of God sent them running?' Elise asked. 'The land seems empty of any threat.'

'Look yonder. Look at that cloud of dust,' one of the men cried out, pointing north.

Where the rolling prairie met the sky, an immense grey cloud rose into the air and, as they watched, the hunters heard a noise like thunder. Then, adding to their growing apprehension, the earth beneath their feet began to tremble. The thunder faded, only to return, sounding louder.

'Whatever it is, it's heading our way,' another man shouted out, his voice cracking with alarm. 'It's certainly not a storm, for the sky is blue.'

No-one replied, for everyone saw at the same moment the landscape seemingly begin to change. Over the nearest crest, a flood of something black in colour swept down towards them, the thunderous roar deafening their ears. Naked fear took hold of the hunters and, as one man, they turned and ran for the streambed. Tumbling into its shelter, Madog stuck his head back over the lip. By now, the black mass was some four hundred paces away and, gasping with amazement, he saw that it consisted of tightly packed animals.

There were thousands of them, all with black, shaggy coats, large heads with wicked horns. They made a fearsome sight. The earth was now visibly shaking under their weight, and Madog knew that the streambed would not protect him and the others. He was about to cry out a warning, when the swiftly approaching leaders of the herd began to swerve to their right. Those following bumped and jostled each other as they did likewise, and to Madog's relief, he saw that they would narrowly miss the ditch. He turned to check that Tudor and Jean were safe and, as he did so, one of the creatures hurtled over his head. The heavy body struck the opposite bank of the streambed with a sickening impact; the beast fell to the ground, kicked convulsively for a few moments, and then lay still.

The stampeding animals took an age to pass but finally, the last of them disappeared across the prairie. Their noise faded away, until only the dust cloud and a wide swathe of trampled grass marked their passage.

'This creature is dead, lads,' one of the men called out, as he prodded the still form with his pike. 'Broken its neck, by the look of it.'

The hunting party gathered around and studied the carcase.

'Looks like some kind of wild cow,' someone remarked. 'I wonder if it tastes the same.'

'Only one way to find out,' another man answered. 'Let's get to work.'

It took them a long while to butcher the warm animal, and Madog suggested that they save the thick, woolly hide.

'We may need it some day,' he said. 'I doubt that summer will last for ever.' While the others worked away, Elise and one of his bowman examined the discarded intestines.

'Are you thinking as I am?' Elise asked, as he held up a length of gut. 'That I am,' the bowman answered, grinning broadly.' Were we to stretch this and dry it out, we would have a fine string for our bows.'

That evening, the crew of the long-ship dined well. They had learned that meat was best when roasted slowly, and they resisted the mouth-watering smell until it was tender. When finally they sat themselves down, each with a generous portion, they tasted buffalo meat for the first time.

Some ten miles up river, Broken Hand, chief of the Sequa tribe, chewed on a mouthful of raw liver. His warriors had had a successful hunt, killing five prime buffalo for the loss of only two of their number. Life was good, and the day to give thanks to The Creator was drawing close.

II

Eric took a last look around the campsite, where the remains of last night's feast littered the ground, and mounds of ashes from the cooking fires scarred the earth. He ensured that the ashes were cold, and then he climbed aboard the long-ship and took his place at the big steering oar. At this point, the Missouri ran deeply and slowly, and on his command, the boat began to move easily up the river. For the first few miles, its course ran more or less straight, until eventually, it took a long left-handed loop. Eric kept the boat close to the right hand bank, where the current was easier, until the loop straightened out. What he saw then caused him to call out in surprise, making the oarsmen look over their shoulders. On the far bank stood a large village made up of beehive shaped huts, amongst which was a number of natives, and as the longboat slowed down, the natives began to run towards an open space, their cries of alarm sounding over the river.

For a while, the oarsmen held the long-ship steady while they eyed the growing crowd, and Eric beckoned to Madog to join him.

'Well, my friend, what do we do now?' he asked. 'I had hoped that we would meet up with the natives, though not as many as those yonder.'

'We have to go to them,' Madog answered. 'We must show that we mean no harm.'

Even as he spoke, the natives began to form themselves into some order, the men pushing the women and children to the rear. Madog could see that the men carried short lances, or bows, though the weapons were not pointing towards the long-ship.

'Steer us across, Eric,' he said. 'Choose five of your strongest men to land with us.' He then called out, 'Rhodri, have five of your pike-men make ready to land. I think it would be wise if we are ready for any trouble.'

Broken Hand stood between The Seer and Buffalo Killer and forced himself not to show his emotions. With a feeling approaching panic, he watched the long-ship draw nearer, its wolf's head pointing directly at him. He sensed the warriors begin to shuffle back and heard Buffalo Killer command them to stand firm. The size of what seemed to him to be a winged boat stunned his brain, and as it drew close, he watched in amazement as the oars, which he had taken for wings, suddenly folded. The boat glided to a halt on the shingle beach, and men leapt over its side. Without a word, they formed a line and walked boldly up to the waiting natives.

Despite himself, Broken Hand took two steps backward, aware that those around him had done the same. Never had he seen such big powerful men. Except for one who was the youngest, the strangers towered head and shoulders above his warriors, and even that youth was taller than Buffalo Killer.

'Who are these giants?' he asked, addressing no-one in particular. He turned to The Seer and asked, 'Has the Creator sent them to us for the ceremony?'

The Seer, who was both spiritual leader and medicine man of the tribe, was completely baffled. The sight of these big strangers, whose hair covered their faces, was beyond his comprehension. He had seen no sign in the flames of his fires, nor in the night sky, which had hinted of their coming. Growing awareness that those around him were waiting with bated breath for his answer, made him decide to play safe.

'Maybe they have been,' he answered. 'I feel that it would do no harm were we to pay them homage.'

'On your knees, my people,' Broken Hand called out, relieved that someone else had made the decision. 'Show your respect to Him who provides for us.'

Norse and Welsh watched in silence as the crowd duly knelt before them.

'By the Gods, I did not expect that!' Eric exclaimed. 'What do we do now?' Madog gave no answer, but he studied the kneeling natives. Their long hair was jet black in colour, their complexion a coppery hue. Except for the three men kneeling directly in front of him, all were dressed in loincloths made of deerskin. The three, who seemed to be in authority, wore sleeveless jackets, adorned with feathers, and fur hats. One of these men stared balefully back at the travellers, the others kept their eyes fixed on the ground. Madog sensed that, if there was going to be any trouble, it would come from that man.

'What do we do, Madog?' Eric asked again.

His friend did not answer, but stepped forward and gently grasped Broken Hand by the shoulders. The chief flinched at his touch and looked fearfully up at him. Madog smiled and urged the chief to his feet before releasing him.

'We come in friendship,' he said, gesturing for all to rise. His words were meaningless to Broken Hand, though, as Madog stood there with his arms extended, his intention was clear enough.

'You were right,' the chief said to The Seer. 'No other tribe has acted like this; they always want to drive us away. These are no ordinary men.' He turned to face the crowd and called out,' Our visitors have truly been sent by The Creator. Make them welcome and give them whatever they desire.' He then commanded his people to disperse, and as they began to move away, he signalled his new guests to come with him. Led by Eric and Madog, the men followed, although now they formed into a tight group, pikes and battle-axes at the ready. Their way led them to the beehive huts, where women and children looked fearfully at them before lowering their gaze. On impulse, Eric made to pick up one little toddler, but its mother snatched the child away and ducked into her hut.

'Best leave them alone for now,' Madog advised his friend. 'Maybe they will not be so scared of us later on.'

The chief finally came to a halt when they came to a circle of open ground, where he motioned his guests to seat themselves in front of a large dwelling. Broken Hand barked out an order, and soon several women appeared, carrying clay pots, which they shared out. The pots held a strong smelling liquid, and Rhodri, who was the first to take a sip, called out. 'By all that is Holy, it tastes better than it smells. It is almost like our ale back home.'

Then, from the ashes of a large fire, the women produced a number of rounded objects, which they shared amongst the visitors. The food smelled delicious and, after breaking the outer skin, Madog and the others had their first taste of the wild potato. By now, The Seer and Buffalo Killer had joined the group, with a score of warriors, who seated themselves a short space away. The warrior chief watched these strange-looking newcomers intently. Their size alone would make them formidable opponents in battle. They were even bigger than those cursed Lakotans, who had driven his tribe from their homeland. He looked with covetous eyes at the weapons they carried. The long lances some of them carried were tipped with something that glistened in the sunlight. Whatever it was, these men had also fashioned it into war axes and long knives. He doubted that his warriors' stone- or bone-headed weapons would last long against theirs. He listened to them talking amongst themselves as they ate, and the surer he became that they were just ordinary men, and not people sent by The Creator. Yet, whoever they were, he dared not speak out, for The Seer was far too powerful to contradict.

When all had eaten, Broken Hand spoke to The Seer.

'I think that now would be the moment to show The Creator's people our offering. They are sure to be pleased with our choice.'

'You speak wisely, as always,' The Seer replied. 'Such beauty will impress them. When they have seen her, they will truly believe that we give Him only the best in thanks.'

Broken Hand spoke to one of his men, who hurried off, to return shortly, accompanied by three women. Two of these plainly belonged to the Sequa tribe, but it was when they saw the third woman that the travellers to fall silent. Tall and slender, dressed only in a deerskin skirt, her raven hair braided at the back, stood the most beautiful girl any one of them had ever seen.

'Show our offering to these people,' the chief commanded.' Let them see her up close.'

'The two women gripped the girl's arms and walked her around the seated men, who gazed in admiration at this lovely vision. The girl was clearly startled at their strange appearance, though, as she passed Madog, she gave him an appealing glance and spoke a few words. Her guardians immediately pushed the girl away, causing her to stumble, and Madog saw that a length of hide bound her ankles together. Before he could move, the girl was hustled away, and Broken Hand approached him.

'She is our sacrifice to The Creator,' he said. 'You must agree that that He will be pleased with such a gift.'

Madog tried desperately to understand, though not one word had any meaning to him and, after a few moments, he merely nodded his head.

'They are pleased with our choice,' Broken Hand called out to the warriors. 'Two more nights and the moon will be full, and then will the ceremony be held.'

The gathering broke up, the travellers returned to the longship, the warriors to their huts. Walking along, Buffalo Killer thought of the girl and her intended fate. In his view, it was a terrible waste of a beauty, who could have been his woman.

Seated in her guarded hut, Laughing Water brushed the tears from her eyes. She was the daughter of War Lance, chief of the Lakotans, the most powerful of the prairie tribes. For the hundredth time, she rued the day that she and her brother had tried to cross the Missouri. Their dugout canoe had overturned in midstream, throwing the two into the fast running current. Somehow, she had managed to hang on to the tiny craft, but there had been no sign of her brother. Mile after mile, she had been swept down river, until she was exhausted and almost unconscious, when the current had cast her onto a shingle beach. How long she lay there, she knew not and she only vaguely remembered the hands that grasped her and dragged her onto the bank. When she regained her senses, it was to find that she was a captive of the hated Sequa. This miserable hut had been her prison for two full moons, almost three. She had no idea what was to become of her, though it surely would not be good.

That night, Madog lay awake for ages. Whenever he closed his eyes, the girl's face filled his mind and he became more and more sure that she was in great danger.

12

The third day following their landing at the village dawned brightly. Madog and the others were astir early, breaking their fast with food supplied by the native women. 'Have you any idea what they are about?' Eric asked, pointing towards the huts. 'Something is going on, and whatever it is, it's going to happen shortly.'

Seated beside him, Madog looked over at the village. The day before, it had been a scene of bustle as numerous bands of Sequa arrived, after making their way over the prairie. He had been with a group of men from the long-ship who had watched one such group arrive. The men had been leading, their women and children, who carried bundles of belongings, followed. What caught the watchers' eyes, though, were the dog-like animals that dragged a wheel-less, loaded platform of poles behind them. As they passed by, the travellers could see that the beasts were similar to the grey wolves back home, their yellow eyes startlingly bright against their coats.

'I know what is missing here,' one of Madog's men said loudly. 'There are no horses. Here we have a land made for riding, and not even an ass to be seen.'

''Tis a strange world, indeed,' another remarked. 'First of all, we met islanders who had no boats, and now we find ourselves in a country that is huge in size but has no animal for a man to ride.'

'Only those wild black beasts, and I do not fancy sitting on one of those,' Rhodri said, with a laugh.

Later that day, Madog had chanced to see the girl again. Flanked by her two guards, she had passed close to him, and had spoken once more in an appealing manner. The two women had pushed her roughly away, their shrill voices scolding the girl. He had watched the trio move on amongst the huts, and again he pondered as to why she was a prisoner. The girl was on his mind all that day and he began to wonder if he could use his strange power over the Sequa to demand her release. That he and his men had some kind of influence over the tribe was without question. Any one of them had only to mime that he needed something and the natives gave it.

The twang of a bowstring brought his mind back to the present moment.

'By the Saints, it truly works well,' he heard Elise cry. 'Come on, lads, try your arm.'

Madog got to his feet and saw the four bowmen standing together on the riverbank.

'These strings are really good, Madog,' Elise called out to him. 'Much stronger than the gut we were trying to use. The warriors also gave a stock of arrows. We are going up-river to try them out.'

With nothing else to attend to, Madog accompanied them and watched as they shot their arrows over the prairie. The bowmen seemed pleased with the result, and debated what their new strings were made of, eventually deciding that they came from an animal's tendon.

When the sun began to dip in the sky, an air of excitement took over the camp. The warriors dressed themselves in feathered finery, and painted their faces and bodies in bright colours. Women began to carry food and drink to the open space in front of Broken Hand's hut. With dusk approaching, drums began to beat, the sounds pulsating over the prairie. Fires were lit, and meat skewered for roasting, while clay pots of the potent drink were handed to the warriors as they arrived. Madog listened to the drums, a strong feeling of apprehension taking hold of him. Eric joined him and, after a few moments, placed a hand on the young man's shoulders.

'What is troubling you?' he asked. 'I have been watching you for a while, and you are plainly worried about something. Our friends in the village seem to be celebrating, and I am sure that they intend us no harm.'

'It is not us that I am worried about,' Madog replied. 'It is the girl I am concerned about. Why are they holding her prisoner? They must have a reason.'

Eric shrugged his shoulders, and then looked over Madog's head.

'I do not know their reason for any of this, though I think that we may be about to find out what it is they are celebrating.'

Madog turned to see Broken Hand and some of his men approaching. The chief looked resplendent in his finery and his face beamed in a smile. He came to a halt, called out some form of greeting, and then gestured to the long-ship's crew to follow him.

'Seems we are being invited to their feast,' Eric said, and had started to call to the others, when Madog bade him stop.

'I fear that something is not quite right,' he told the Norseman. 'We shall accept the invitation, but I want every man armed.' He saw Eric raise his brow in surprise and added,' I cannot tell your men to do so, Eric, but the Welsh will be taking their weapons.'

While the Norse leader spoke with his men, Madog called to the two lads, who ran to his side.

'I want you to stay here and guard the boat,' he told them. 'Whatever happens, do not let a single native get on board.'

Though disappointed, the lads saw the earnest look on his face and, without question, scrambled aboard.

Broken Hand waited in silence as the travellers prepared to follow him. That they now carried their weapons came as a surprise, though he had no choice but to accept the fact. With another sweep of his arm, he led off, threading a way through the huts. When they reached the space in front of his hut, he motioned his guests to be seated. Madog saw that the open ground had been transformed. At a guess, close on three hundred warriors now sat in ranks, to form a semicircle. Cooking fires burned brightly in the gathering gloom, while women moved about, refilling pots with drink. It all seemed harmless enough, until his eyes focussed on an object directly opposite to where he sat. By the light of a fire, he saw that a large stake had been driven into the earth, and he felt a chill run down his spine. He now knew for certain why the girl was a captive.

Seated between Rhodri and Eric, he spoke with each man, voicing his fears.

'The girl is to be sacrificed,' he told them. 'I am not going to let that happen.' He turned to Elise, who sat behind him, and told him, 'I want you to be ready to shoot. Aim true, when I tell you, my friend. Your target will be clear enough.'

By now, a full moon had begun to rise in the night sky, and was bathing the village in its pale light. The drumbeats grew faster, until they became frenzied, the warriors swaying wildly to their sound. It was then that Madog saw the girl. Held by two warriors, Laughing Water was dragged out of the hut closest to the stake. Despite her struggles, within moments, she was tied securely to it. The girl was obviously aware of her intended fate, and tried desperately to free herself. Only when The Seer appeared and walked towards her did she cease to resist. The medicine man raised a hand high and the wild drumming ceased. A silence, broken only by the girl's sobs, fell over the gathering. The Seer halted, raised his face to the moon, and with his voice quavering with emotion, he called out a short incantation. He then stood quite still for a while, before he turned, towards the girl; with a knife held high in his hand, he stepped close to her.

Madog leapt to his feet. 'Kill him, Elise,' he shouted, and began to sprint across the open space. He heard the rush of air as an arrow flashed past him, and saw it strike The Seer between the shoulders. The man spun around, dropped the knife and slumped to the ground. Madog leaped over the still form, his sword at the ready. The two warriors were still flanking the girl, not moving, their mouths open in surprise. Only when Buffalo Killer's ringing cry of anger sounded did they begin to move. Another arrow zipped past Madog, and he saw one of the warriors fall flat, the shaft buried deep in his chest. Frantically, he slashed at the girl's bonds. Hearing her shout of warning, he spun round, somehow blocking a swinging club with the blade of his sword. The blade bit into the warrior's arm and, as he jerked back in pain, Madog thrust his sword into the lithe body. With one last cut, he freed the girl and, supporting her with his free arm, he turned towards to his men. With relief, he saw that they were already rushing towards him, forming a rough circle as they did so.

'Bring her inside,' Eric yelled. 'You guard her well. Leave the rest to us. 'Listen to me, lads,' he called to the others. 'Make for the long-ship. Should any man bar your path, cut him down.'

So quickly had Madog and the men acted, that the warriors were still seated, but now, Buffalo Killer's voice made them move. Beside himself with rage, the warrior chief ran into the centre of the open ground. Few of his men were armed, and he screamed at the others to get their bows and spears. He could see that it would be hopeless for the few to attack these white men, as he called them, and he forced himself to wait.

Somehow keeping their protective circle around the girl, the Norse and Welsh made their way through the huts. The moon lit their way and soon they saw the familiar shape of their boat at its mooring. Behind them, warriors began whooping their war cries, the sounds drawing closer with every passing moment. Once down on the shingle, the men began to scramble aboard,

Madog hoisting the girl up to the two boys. Arrows began to thump into the timber deck and a Norseman fell, cursing with pain, an arrow in his thigh. Some of Eric's men reached under the rowing benches and began to hand out the heavy wooden shields that were stored there. A few shadowy figures jumped from the bank and made towards the boat, only to be skewered by Rhodri's pike-men. Safely aboard, Elise and the other bowmen loosed at the warriors outlined on the bank, two of their targets falling, while the rest vanished.

'Get aboard now, Rhodri,' Madog yelled, at which, the pike-men hurled themselves upward and over the boat's side. More arrows struck the craft, and another man fell, with a strangled cry, a shaft in his throat. With a swing of his axe, Eric cut the mooring rope as the last man scrambled over the side. The long-ship began to move, and some of the men grabbed their oars, while others held their shields, to cover them. Torberg joined Eric at the steering oar, holding a protecting shield over his captain's head. Slowly the oars began to bite into the current, and Eric steered for the far bank, to escape the stinging arrows, The long-ship had almost reached the deeper water, when a number of fiery lights shot from the bank. The lights arced gracefully through the sky and dropped suddenly on and around the boat.

'Fire arrows,' a man yelled in warning. Several of the crew began to free the burning shafts, tossing them overboard, but they had to seek cover as another hail of fire arrows descended. It was then that the inevitable happened: a number landed on the rolled up sail and, immediately, the dry cloth caught fire, and flames raced along its length. Try as they might, no man could get near the flames, which drove everyone to the bow or stern. The long-ship quickly lost way and began to spin around in the current. The fire took hold of the bone-dry woodwork, and it was with a feeling of deep despair that Eric knew that his beloved boat was now doomed. He became aware that the crew were now looking at him, and in a voice choking with grief, he gave the order to abandon the long-ship. The heat was so intense that no man needed urging; everyone jumped over the side into the chest deep water. The Sequa warriors' cries of triumph filled the night and despite, Buffalo Killers' command for them to stay, a number dashed into the river.

Arrows were still falling on and around the blazing long-ship, and now Rhodri took command. Bracing himself against the flow, he formed the men with shields into a line, placing his pike-men and the others behind them. The Sequa kept coming, until the water came up to their chins. The wretched warriors were now more or less helpless, and Rhodri ordered his men to pass through the line of shields. In moments, the swords and battle-axes had done their work, turning the river into a place of carnage. Those warriors lucky enough to escape the slaughter fled back to the bank, where they faced the wrath of their chief.

Rhodri quickly reformed the men, and then looked toward Madog, awaiting an order. For once, the young man had no idea what to do. Were they to attempt a crossing of the river, they risked drowning, which left only two options. They could force their way upstream, or take the easier way and go with the current. He was still undecided, when the girl grabbed his arm. Her lovely face no longer had a look of fear, but showed a savagery that startled the young Welshman. He saw that she now held a sword dropped by one of the stricken men. She shouted something in her native tongue. When Madog made no response, Laughing Water shook him violently and pointed northwards.

'The girl wants us to head upstream,' he called to Rhodri. 'I have no idea where it will lead us, though I feel sure that we can trust her.'

'Upstream, or down, it matters not,' the soldier yelled back. 'We must move from here quickly. We are easy targets, standing here. Get Eric to shift, will you.' Madog looked around him and saw that his friend was standing alone. Eric seemed unaware of the arrows falling around him as he watched the long-ship drift downstream. The boat was now burning fiercely, and as Madog waded towards the big Norseman, the mast crashed down and caused the boat to capsize. Gently but firmly, Madog took hold of Eric and began to lead him away.

'Come away, my friend, there is nothing you can do. The men need you with them,' he said.

Eric took one last look at the burning wreck and nodded.

'This New World will have to be our new home, Madog,' he said. 'There is no way back for us now.'

Led by Rhodri, the men began to move upriver, helping their wounded and the two lads to fight the current. Twice more the Sequa's arrows found their target, both men slipping beneath the surface. Gamely, the Welsh and Norse struggled on until, eventually, the arrows ceased. On the riverbank, Buffalo Killer commanded his warriors to return to the village. Most of them had drunk too much of the bitter brew, earlier on, and he wanted them sober by daylight. There was no hurry, there was no hiding place on the prairie for these white men.

Slowly but surely, the men of the long-ship made their way upstream. At first, despite the hail of arrows stopping, Rhodri feared a trap, and kept to the river. Only much later, when their limbs were aching with the strain and the cold, did he lead them ashore. When all were safely on the bank, he formed them into a defensive circle and then spoke with Madog.

'We were lucky to get away with such a small loss,' he said. 'What now? Do we continue north?'

Madog looked for the girl to confirm that this was what she wanted. He found her and the two lads rubbing vigorously at their legs, in an attempt to restore warmth. When he pointed north, she nodded her agreement and then spoke, indicating

Tudor and Jean. Aware that he did not understand, she placed a hand on her breast and quickly pointed in that direction. Once clear in his mind what the girl intended, Madog nodded and spoke to the two lads.

'The girl wants you to go with her,' he told them. 'Do what she wants and take care of her for me.' He saw that Raoul was watching them, and explained to the Breton what the girl intended. 'Both lads will be safer away from here,' he added. Raoul held his son close for a few moments, speaking softly to the lad, and then stood back. Laughing Water gripped the Breton's arm, trying to assure him that all would be well, before she turned away, and, followed by the two lads, began to run north.

By now, both boys were superbly fit, and easily kept up with the girl. They had run only some fifty paces, however, when she slowed to a walk. Fifty paces more and she broke into another run, repeating the action until the moonlight faded. Lit only by the stars, they walked quickly, their feet swishing through the prairie grass. When at length the sky eastwards began to brighten, Laughing Water began to run again. On and on they travelled, running and then walking. How many miles they had covered could only be guessed at, though, by now, both lads were beginning to feel weary. The girl sensed this and urged them on, only halting when the sun was quite high in the sky. The two sank to the ground at her signal that they should rest, though she remained standing, her eyes searching south for any sign of pursuit.

After a while, Laughing Water gestured them to rise and once more set off. The vastness of the land seemed to swallow them up, and Tudor thought that they were like three tiny ants crossing the sands around Moel-y-Gest. The girl's stamina amazed both lads.

'She could outrun the pony I had back home,' Tudor gasped, at one stage, 'though I would gladly give a King's ransom to have him here right now.'

'So would I,' Jean puffed out. 'that is, if he was big enough to carry the pair of us.'

Another brief stop and they were off again. The only feeling they had of making progress was whenever they reached a low rise in the earth, from which they could look back over the empty miles to another rise, which they had passed earlier. The sun had passed noon when yet another rise appeared in the distance. Nothing marked this rise from any of those that they had already passed; but Laughing Water became agitated, forcing the pace. Neither of the lads could keep up with her, and she called something to them, a smile of joy lighting her face. With a signal to follow her, she ran on ahead and disappeared over the crest. When she reached the downward slope, the girl paused for a moment, to take in the familiar scene. The line of aspen trees, which followed a tributary of the Missouri, broke the endless prairie, while the village of the Lakotans nestled close to them. Laughing Water had finally returned home. People were moving about the lodges, and, giving a high-pitched whoop, she ran down the slope.

Her arrival was met at first with looks of disbelief, which were soon replaced by cries of joy. Within moments, she was in the centre of a laughing crowd, who touched her gently, as though to re-assure themselves that the new arrival was truly Laughing Water.

'Let me through,' a commanding voice rang out. The crowd parted to allow a tall, well-built man to pass through them. When he saw the girl, he halted and raised both his arms.

'It truly is you, daughter,' he cried out. 'The great Manitou has brought you safely back to us.'

The girl ran up to him, and he embraced her in a crushing hug.

'I feared that you were dead, little one,' he said tenderly. War

Lance felt his daughter sway when he released his grip, and held her at arm's length, bidding one of those in the crowd to fetch water. The girl drank sparingly, then pointed back towards the rise, where the two lads now stood.

'They are two young warriors, father,' she explained. 'They are of the tribe that saved my life. Bring them down here and make them welcome.'

Tudor and Jean sat in the long grass, their legs shaking with fatigue.

'I'm frightened, Tudor,' Jean said fearfully as they watched the scene below. 'What will they do to us?'

Tudor swallowed hard when he saw two warriors head towards them at a trot.

'Make us welcome, of course,' he answered, in an anxious tone. 'All we can do is wait and see. I simply cannot run another step.'

They watched the approaching warriors in silence, then, with relief, when they saw that the two men were smiling at them. One of the warriors said something to them, bent low, scooped up Jean, and cradled him in his powerful arms. The other native did the same with Tudor, and then they began to stride down to the village. Meanwhile, Laughing Water had told her father of the Sequa's' attempt to sacrifice her, and of the plight of those who had saved her. War Lance's face darkened in anger.

'Then, we must go to their aid,' he snapped. 'Go, arm yourselves, you warriors of the Lakotans,' he called out. 'Those who saved Laughing Water are in danger. We are in honour bound to help them.'

The men immediately ran to their lodges, to reappear carrying bows or lances. 'My friends will be following the river, father,' the girl told him. 'Make haste, I beg you. Their leader is a young warrior with a noble look, and his safety means everything to me.'

By now, the two lads had joined her, and the three watched the war band form up and then set off at a trot up to and over the crest.

'Come, let us eat and rest for now,' Laughing Water said to the lads, with a warm smile. 'You have more than earned both this day.'

13

'Come on, come on, you heathens,' Rhodri growled, as he dodged behind a Norseman's shield. 'A little closer, my friends, and you will feel the edge of my sword.'

He glanced quickly about him, to make sure that the circle of men was unbroken. All of them, except for Eric, were sheltering from the arrows loosed by the Sequa warriors. Wearing his helmet and carrying a shield and battle-axe, the giant Norse leader stood upright, taunting his foe. Now and then, an arrow would speed towards him, and, with a contemptuous movement, he would flick it aside with his shield. Rhodri could see that the big man was aching to get to grips with their enemy, and he turned once more to his front and judged that now was the moment.

'Get ready,' he yelled, and gave the order to charge. 'Rush them, lads. Hit them hard.'

At his command, Elise's bowmen loosed their arrows at the nearest Sequa warriors. The Norsemen dropped their shields and, with Rhodri's pike-men in the lead, rushed headlong at their foe. The speed of their charge took the natives by surprise and, before they could turn away, the white men were amongst them. Warriors screamed as the pikes pierced them; the weight of the charging men bowled over others, who were never to rise again after swords and axes had done their deadly work. A few of the bravest warriors fought back, swinging their stone clubs, and a pike-man fell, his skull crushed like an eggshell. His death added to his comrades' fury, and they fought like crazy men, showing no mercy. Eric whirled his battle-axe and struck down a warrior foolish enough to tackle him. Finally outmatched by superior weapons and the size of their opponents, the Sequa fell back, slowly at first, and then in full flight.

Their chests heaving from the strain of battle, the men of the long-ship watched the Sequa go.

'They will keep their distance after that,' Madog gasped, wiping his bloodied sword in the grass. 'It will soon be nightfall; until then, Elise, keep those warriors away with your bows as best you can.'

Elise, who was collecting fallen arrows, nodded in reply. He and his bowmen had been shooting most of that day, and their arms now ached painfully. The Sequa had quickly learned the power of their longbows, and, on Buffalo Killer's command, had kept their distance. While the bulk of his warriors shadowed the white men, the chief had small groups run in closer, shoot their arrows and then run back. Only now had he led his main force against his foe. The move had cost the Sequa dear, for more than a score of their number lay in the trampled prairie grass. When his men had regrouped, Buffalo Killer led them off, keeping pace with the white men. He no longer watched them closely, but kept looking ahead, finally seeing what he had hoped for. Some distance ahead of him, the earth began to rise gently, before lifting sharply, to form a ridge. The ridge was less than a hundred feet in height, but, with one end anchored on the river, it ran for miles across the prairie. With a cry of triumph, he broke into a run and, followed by his warriors, made for this natural barrier. When they eventually reached the top, he formed his men into a line facing south. He could see that the white men were still a long way off, and, as he watched, he saw them come to a halt.

'The tricky devils,' Madog exclaimed, when he saw the natives forming a line on the ridge. 'It is going to be hard work, driving them off that hill. What do you think, Rhodri? Do we attack them now?'

The soldier studied the ridge for a while, and then shook his head.

'Not now, Madog,' he finally answered. 'It has been a testing day and the men are bone weary. We must rest for now, and tackle them at dawn.'

Later, as darkness fell, Eric spoke with Madog and asked the question which was on every man's mind. 'Do you truly believe that the girl has gone for help?'

'I do, my friend. I am wagering our lives that she has,' Madog answered.

At daybreak, Madog bade the men make ready. Few needed urging, for most had spent a restless night, thinking of what fate had in store for them. With Eric at his side, the young man led off, heading directly for the ridge and the waiting Sequa. As the gap narrowed, Madog saw that where the ridge reached the river, it plunged steeply into the water. A glimmer of hope swept through him, and, as they began to climb toward the ridge, he told Eric what he had in mind. The Norseman nodded, and together they called back to their men. Side by side, the two broke into a run, suddenly swinging to their right, and when they reached the river, they began to climb quickly up the ridge.

Their move caught Buffalo Killer by surprise. His warriors had spread along the ridge, and now he yelled at them to group, to meet this new threat. His men jostled and pushed each other as they tried to obey his command, becoming a disorganised, mob. Not waiting for a command, Elise and his men loosed their arrows at the easy target now presented to them. Warriors fell, clutching at the shafts that had pierced their bodies, and were trampled under foot. For a few moments, the Sequa wavered, many looking over their shoulders for ways of escape. They found none, for more warriors were now reaching the end of the ridge, which quickly became a heaving mass of men.

It was now that Buffalo Killer took his place at their head.

The nearest white man was only some five paces below him, and, with a whooping war cry, he charged down at his foe. With the advantage of the higher ground, the chief swung his stone club at Madog. The young man ducked low, and the club whirled harmlessly over his head. Madog drove the point of his sword, upwards, but the chief swerved aside, and the blade grazed his arm. The next moment, both men were locked together in combat, only to be bowled over when the bunched up warriors struck them. The impact caused Madog to loosen his grip on his sword, and he lost sight of it amongst the flattened grass.

He saw Buffalo Killer get to his knees and begin to swing his club, and, desperately, Madog threw himself at the chief. Locked together once more, the two rolled down the slope, each intent on killing the other and oblivious to the fighting raging around them. Somehow, Buffalo Killer broke free and, with a whoop of triumph, got to his feet, his club held high. His mouth twisted in hatred, he glared down at the young Welshman and began to bring the club down. Madog raised both arms in feeble defence and waited for the blow. It never came for, as though by magic, a bloodied arrowhead appeared in Buffalo Killer's chest. For a moment, the chief stood still, a look of disbelief on his face, and then he fell forward.

'One of my better shots,' Elise yelled above the din, as he helped Madog to his feet. 'Luckily, I stood well clear of the fight, otherwise I would not have seen you. You had best get yourself another weapon and quickly. Things are not looking good.' This was true enough. Madog now saw that the men of the long-ship were being forced down the slope. Once on the even ground, they would lose the cliff's protection on their right flank, and be surrounded. A Norseman lay close by, and Madog picked up the man's discarded battleaxe. Elise placed his bow by the still form and, drawing his sword, followed Madog up to the battle. The Sequa were now sensing victory and, despite their losses, pressed home their attack. Madog could see Eric and Rhodri fighting shoulder to shoulder, and many of the Sequa swerving aside to avoid them. It was then that Madog saw more warriors appear on the ridge above. With a sinking heart, he watched them begin to run down to the fight, only realising at the last moment that the newcomers looked different from the Sequa. Their lances at the ready, the strange warriors ran full tilt into Buffalo Killer's men. The shouts of triumph quickly turned to that of alarm, and then fear, as the Sequa reeled under the charge. In moments, the scene changed dramatically. Caught now between two enemy forces, the Sequa began to break away. Those at the rear, recognising their new foe, made no attempt to fight back, but simply ran for the open prairie, to be followed by the remainder, as panic took hold. A number of War Lance's men chased after them, whooping their war cries, while the others stood amongst the fallen, staring at the white men.

'The girl has played her part well,' Madog gasped, as he joined Eric and Rhodri. 'When you asked me last night what I thought she would do, I must admit that I was not really sure what she was about.'

Joined by Elise, they waited for the new warriors to make a move, noting with relief that they seemed friendly enough. Eventually, a single warrior came up to them and spoke briefly. Madog indicated that he did not understand and War Lance smiled and shrugged his powerful shoulders. He called out to his warriors, at which, they began to help the white men who were wounded. When satisfied that all were being aided, he signed to Madog to follow him and began to walk northwards. The party travelled slowly, tending to the injured as they crossed the prairie, arriving at the village two days later. Here, the two lads greeted them joyously and Jean said a silent prayer of thanks for his father's survival. Amongst the happy crowd, Madog caught sight of Laughing Water. Their eyes met and they smiled at each other. The girl pushed through the throng and threw her arms around the young man, who held her close. Rhodri looked at the happy couple for a while, and then turned to Eric.

'I believe our travels are finally over, my friend,' he said, with a broad smile on his face.

14

1840 A.D.

Caleb Evans brought his horse to a stop and looked down at the Missouri. The guide rope tied about his waist fell slack, and he knew that 'Old Wall Eye', his pack mule, had also come to a halt. Downstream, the river looped away, as he vaguely remembered it, as it ran towards St. Louis. To his front was the place where the village should be standing, the village that he and Zeb Carter had visited, so many years ago. Now, however, all that remained of the lodges were mounds of earth and logs, creating a picture of desolation.

Gently tapping his hide boots on the horse's flanks, Caleb began to move down the gentle slope, feeling the guide rope tighten. With a sigh, he looked back at 'Old Wall Eye', who glared back at him. Caleb never knew if the mule was playing a game, or if the animal was just plain awkward. Which ever it was, it happened every time that he wanted to move on. He gave the rope a fierce tug, and the mule reluctantly began to follow him.

As he rode down, Caleb thought back over the years since his first visit to this place. Zeb no longer roamed the prairie, or the far off mountains, in search of furs. Four winters back, he had died peacefully in his sleep, lying close to Caleb. His passing had left the younger man with a terrible emptiness, and Caleb had decided, there and then, to return to civilisation. Such was his love of the wilderness, however, that it had taken him four years to get this far east.

He thought of Morning Star, whom he had met here, and looked over to his left. Beyond the low rise lay the stream that he and the girl had bathed in, a place of happy memories. During the past twenty years of trapping, he had stayed at many Indian camps and been friendly with many maidens, yet the memory of his first encounter with an Indian tribe remained the clearest in his mind.

It was then that he felt the hairs on the back of his neck rise. Outlined against the rise, an Indian sat on his pony watching the trapper. When Caleb reached the first of the ruined lodges, he stopped and dismounted, all the while keeping his eyes on the distant figure. To his surprise, the lone rider began to move down towards him, keeping his mount at a steady walk.

Unsure of the Indian's intention, Caleb moved around his horse, placing it between himself and the oncoming rider. Slowly, he pulled his almost new musket from its saddle bucket and primed the pan, leaving the gun un-cocked. The musket had a rifled barrel and was accurate up to three hundred yards, bringing the Indian well within its reach. The warrior, however, made no hostile move but drew close, halted his horse and raised a hand in the sign of peace. Still holding his gun at the ready, Caleb stepped out into the open and responded with a similar signal. The warrior cut a fine picture of a Plains Indian as he sat his wiry pony. Dressed only in a breechclout and moccasins, he carried a feathered war-lance and a small, brightly painted shield. His raven-coloured hair hung in two thick braids over his shoulders, and Caleb recognised the man as being a member of the powerful Sioux nation. 'Peace between us,' Caleb called out in Lakotan, upon which, the Indian slid lithely to the ground and walked closer.

'Peace between us,' he replied in kind, and looked around at the crumbled lodges. 'A sad sight, white man,' he said. 'This place was once a happy one, full of love and laughter. Now, it is but home to many spirits.'

Caleb studied the warrior as he talked, guessing that he was about twenty years old. His skin was lightly tanned and his features were small boned, and Caleb knew that he was a half-breed, part Indian, part white. There was something about the other man's looks that bothered Caleb, but what it was he could not figure out.

'You are a long way from home,' he said eventually.' What brings you here?' The warrior turned to face him, and said, 'This is where I was born. I lived here for five winters, as a child. Then, one summer, some white men passed through and stayed for one night. Some days afterwards, our people began to be ill. Many died, their bodies covered with sores. My mother fled, taking me north, to join our cousins, the Teton Sioux. I have come here simply to see my birth place.'

'How are you called?' Caleb asked.

'Running Horse,' the warrior answered. 'I race other braves for a gamble. I mostly win.'

'And your mother, how is she called?' Caleb asked.

'Morning Star,' came the answer.

For a few moments, Caleb was struck dumb, his mind reeling.

'She is well?' he finally blurted out.

'Well enough,' Running Horse answered, 'though she is grieving the loss of her man, White Cloud. He was killed in a war with the Crow tribe, five moons ago,'

Caleb looked for a long time at the young warrior and knew he was his son. Then, he swung himself up into the saddle.

'I must ride on to St. Louis,' he said. 'Where will your people be, come winter?'

'In the sacred Black Hills,' Running Horse promptly answered. 'We always camp there when the great cold comes.'

'Then, tell your mother that Caleb, the trader, the man she called 'Cariad', will meet her there. Tell her that he will take care of her,' Caleb said.

He raised a hand in farewell, nudged his horse forward, and rode down river. For once, 'Old Wall Eye' placidly followed.